THE HALO WIND

THE HALO WIND

Judith St. George

G.P. Putnam's Sons, New York

Copyright © 1978 by Judith St. George
All rights reserved. Published
simultaneously in Canada by
Longman Canada Limited, Toronto.
Printed in the United States of America

Library of Congress Cataloging in Publication Data

St. George, Judith
    The halo wind.

    SUMMARY: A young girl begins to wonder if a Chinook
companion is causing or alleviating hardships a group
of pioneers experiences on its way to Oregon.
    [1.   Overland journeys to the Pacific—Fiction.
2.   Chinook Indians—Fiction.   3.   Indians of North
America—Fiction]   I.   Title.
PZ7.S142Han   [Fic]   78-16640
ISBN 0-399-20651-5

Second Impression

THE HALO WIND

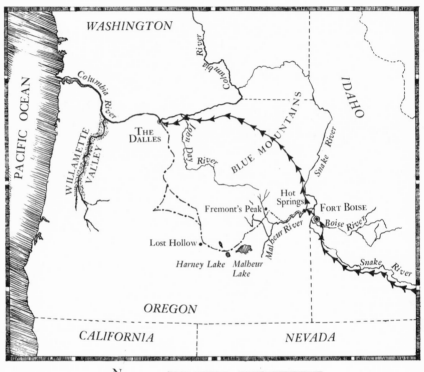

WASHINGTON

PACIFIC OCEAN

Columbia River

Columbia River

IDAHO

WILLAMETTE VALLEY

THE DALLES

John Day River

BLUE MOUNTAINS

Snake River

Fremont's Peak

Hot Springs

FORT BOISE

Boise River

Lost Hollow

Malheur River

Harney Lake   Malheur Lake

Snake River

OREGON

CALIFORNIA

NEVADA

N

W   E

S

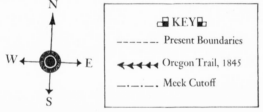

KEY

- - - - - - - Present Boundaries

◄◄◄◄◄ Oregon Trail, 1845

- · - · - · - Meek Cutoff

CHAPTER ONE

I LAY ON MY MATTRESS STARING UP at the campfire shadows dancing on the wagon cover. Ma and Pa were arguing right outside the wagon. Though my mother and father didn't always think alike, I couldn't ever remember them quarreling like they were now, and their angry voices kept me awake.

"Stephen Meek knows this country like the palm of his hand." Pa was almost shouting. "His cutoff bypasses most of the Columbia River and the Blue Mountains altogether."

"How can you even consider not following the regular trail? You know Ella Jane's leg isn't mending properly. She needs to

9

be settled, so she can rest and let it heal the way it should." Ma's voice was low, but it carried clearly.

"Ella Jane's one of the reasons I *am* considering the cutoff," Pa retorted. "Meek told me it's a hundred and fifty miles shorter than the old road. We'd reach The Dalles days before the rest of the wagons."

Ella Jane Thatcher. That was me they were talking about and my leg that I'd hurt five weeks ago. I was thirteen, and the youngest of the Thatcher family. We'd been on the road to the Oregon country since May of this year, 1845. Now it was August, and we were camped at Fort Boise, just four hundred miles from the Willamette Valley where we were headed. Now some of the men were talking about taking a cutoff from the known Oregon road.

"Don't use Ella Jane as an excuse, John," Ma scolded. "You know as well as I do that you hanker for anything new, no matter how hard it is on the rest of us."

I had never heard Ma speak up so strongly, not even when Pa had moved us from Ohio to Illinois three years ago, then from Illinois out here to the Oregon country. It worried me that Ma was so upset about taking the cutoff. Though Ma was strict and hard sometimes, she had a common sense that I trusted. I didn't want to take the cutoff either.

We had taken a cutoff once before, with twenty other wagons. That was when I'd hurt my leg. The road was steep, and I'd been helping push the wagon when I'd slipped and fallen, twisting my leg so bad I thought it was broken. Doctor Wilcox was traveling with the main caravan, so Pa had straightened my leg the best he could and splinted it with a wagon spoke. The pain had been so terrible, I hardly remembered the three days it had taken us to catch up to the other wagons. Then, when Doctor Wilcox looked at my leg, he decided it was dislocated, not broken. He had to straighten and splint it all over again. It still hurt now, but nothing like it had those awful days after the accident.

I realized the argument outside the wagon wasn't over. Now my brother Addis had joined in. "Meek's lived in this country for fifteen years, Ma, and he piloted us safe from Missouri to Fort Hall. If I had a say, I'd vote for his cutoff, too." Handsome, six feet tall, with copper red hair like no one else in the family, Addis was sixteen and itching to be looked on as a man.

"Well, you don't have a say, Addis, and for that matter, neither does your mother," Pa declared. "This is my decision and mine alone. I'll take everything into account, then judge what's best for the family."

"But Mattie and Henry are taking the old road," Ma protested.

"I'll hear no more about it, Hester," Pa cut her right off.

That was something I hadn't even considered. My sister Mattie was being married at the fort tomorrow, and she and Henry must have already made plans to travel with the Jenkins' wagon on the regular road. I just couldn't bear to be separated from Mattie, too. We had left Grandma Fleming behind in Ohio, and my brother Benton and his bride behind on their farm in Illinois. My oldest sister Lucy, her husband and two babies had been the hardest of all to leave . . .

"Chuck, chuck, chuck."

It was Sparky, chirping away in her cage. Ma and Pa's arguing must have awakened her, too. Sparky was my darling pet, a desert chipmunk Pa had caught for me when I hurt my leg. I had tamed her so she answered to my call. I took her tobacco tin cage off the shelf and sprinkled some mustard seeds in my lap.

"Tsst. Tsst. Tsst." I clicked my tongue against the roof of my mouth in our special signal and unlatched her cage door. First I heard her soft chirp, then I felt her step onto my leg. She paused, then scurried up my leg until she reached the seeds in my lap. Without hesitating, she sat right up on her hind legs and began to groom herself. She moistened her forepaws with her tongue and washed her face and ears so fast I could hardly follow her motions. I was pleased. Sparky had never felt comfortable enough with me before to groom herself on my lap.

When she was finished, she began to stuff the seeds first into one cheek pouch, then the other. I laughed. Sparky carried so much food back to her storeroom tin, I had to empty it out from time to time when she was sleeping. I offered her the same nuts and seeds all over again, and she happily hid them away as if she had never seen them before.

All of a sudden, she sat up on her hind legs and gave a shrill whistle of alarm. Unexpected motion frightened Sparky and someone was noisily opening the wagon cover. It was Ma and Mattie coming into the wagon to get dressed for the night. I carefully slipped Sparky back into her cage. Her little nails scratched across the tin floor as she scampered back to her corner nest. Sparky was a comfort to me, and I loved her.

"Shh," I heard Ma whisper. "Ella Jane's asleep."

"No, I'm not," I called out.

"Well, you should be. It's late."

"Is anything settled, Ma?" Mattie asked as she unbuttoned her dress. "Did you talk Pa into taking the old route with Henry and me?"

"Your father knows how I feel about it, Mattie. I can't do anything more than that." Ma slipped her nightgown over her clothes, then somehow got her dress off from underneath it. I had never figured out how she did it so neatly.

"I got to admit, it's more than just following a new route that bothers me," Ma went on. "I'm not sure I trust that Mr. Meek. Look at how he up and married that seventeen-year-old girl last May a week after meeting her. It's only his word we got that he knows the territory."

That was something else I hadn't thought of. "If Mr. Meek is the only one who knows the way, Ma, what if he got sick or hurt so he couldn't lead the wagons?" I asked.

Ma unpinned her knot of gray hair so it fell down over her shoulders. "It's not your concern, Ella Jane, and there's no sense fretting about it. Your father doesn't have to make a decision about the cutoff until we reach the hot springs in three days, so forget it for the time being."

The three of us fell silent. No matter what Ma said, I was thinking about the cutoff. As for Ma, I never knew what was on her mind, but I was sure Mattie was thinking about her wedding tomorrow. She was brushing her hair so hard it crackled in the dry, cold air. Mattie was vain about her hair, and her looks, too. Why shouldn't she be? She was eighteen and beautiful, with round pink cheeks and brook-blue eyes. Her biggest worry all across the continent had been how the sun and wind were burning and chapping her fair skin. Mattie and I were different in every way. I thought of my own dark skin and brown eyes and dark, straight hair. I was small for my age, too, instead of tall like Mattie.

Mattie abruptly stopped brushing her hair. "Wouldn't it be terrible if all those Indians camping around the fort came to my wedding?" Since meeting Henry, Mattie had tried to keep the whine out of her voice, but every once in a while, like now, it crept back in.

I couldn't help laughing. "They can come only if they dress up proper, Mattie," I teased.

"Humph, if it was your wedding, you'd probably invite every savage in sight," Mattie snapped.

Mattie and I were different that way, too. She didn't have much use for Indians, but I thought they were fascinating. All across the country, Indians had watched our caravan pass by, and I had watched the Indians. Even now we could hear the chanting from the Indian wigwam village just beyond Fort Boise. Pa said the Indian men sometimes chanted and beat wooden sticks in rhythm all night playing some kind of gambling game.

"You just don't understand that Indians are special, Mattie . . ." I began.

"Now you girls hush," Ma ordered. "It's past eleven. Tomorrow's a busy day, and we got to be rested for it." Ma's voice was final sounding, and I knew she'd tolerate no more talking.

I lay awake long after Ma and Mattie had settled down in their tents outside. I slept on a mattress in the wagon only because it was more comfortable than a blanket roll. I rubbed my aching leg. It always seemed to hurt more after a long day's jouncing in the springless wagon. Or maybe it was because the temperature had dropped at least thirty degrees since sunset and the cold bothered it.

Outside I heard Pa and Addis settle down for the night, too. Then I listened to the restless camp noises that never ceased, the lowing and shuffling of the livestock, dogs barking, a man and his wife talking, a baby crying out in his sleep, coughing and snoring, the gurgle of the Snake River not far away, and in the distance, the Indians' chanting.

I was almost asleep when I heard the coyote. After three months on the road, I thought I'd heard every kind of coyote call there was, yips and yaps, barks and snorts, wails and squeals and howls. But this one was so different, it jolted me awake. His piercing cry was almost a song, rising and falling like a human voice.

It was a startling reminder that we were in wild, unsettled country, hundreds of miles from anything familiar. There were hundreds and hundreds of us emigrating west together. Our numbers were our only protection. Now Pa was thinking of separating us from the main caravan on a cutoff. As I listened to the strange coyote song, the notion of traveling even deeper into unknown wilderness chilled me right to the marrow. Shivering, I pulled my warm quilt tight around me.

CHAPTER TWO

THE WEDDING WAS ALMOST OVER.
Though the ceremony was being held in the biggest room of the fort, there were so many people pressed in to watch, it was terribly hot. Flies buzzed against the tiny windows as the parson in his shiny black suit finished sermonizing. I looked over at Pa. He had tears in his eyes. Tears came easy to Pa, just like to me. There were no tears in Ma's eyes. Her back was straight as a poker and she had knotted her gray hair so tight, her skin was stretched shiny over her cheekbones.

". . . and live together in holy love until your lives' end. Amen."

It was done. Mattie was married to her skinny, already balding Henry Jenkins. Sudden tears filled my eyes, too. There would be no more taffy pulls with Mattie at Christmastime, and no more hunting for wild strawberries on early June mornings either. I watched Pa give Mattie a squeeze and a kiss as he shook Henry's hand. Pa was laughing now, the tears gone. Ma stepped forward, too. She pressed her cheek first against Mattie's face, then against Henry's.

"Welcome to the family," she murmured.

By the time I had kissed Mattie and Henry, Pa had pulled out the whiskey jug he kept hidden under the false floor of our wagon.

"To Mr. and Mrs. Jenkins," he toasted. He took a swallow from the jug and offered it to Mr. Craigie, the supervisor of the fort. Mr. Craigie was a short Scotsman with a ruddy red face who took only a short drink before he handed the jug on to the next man. No one took more than a quick swallow before passing it on. Whiskey was saved for fever and toothache and broken bones. Pa had given me whiskey when I'd hurt my leg and I could still feel the burn of it going down my throat. Then it was Addis' turn. He held up the jug longer than anyone. I glanced at Ma. She was watching Addis, too, and frowning.

I shifted my weight on my crutches. Ma had lined them with lamb's wool, but my underarms were tender and sore, and my leg ached from standing so long. I edged over to the door and leaned against it. Old Mr. Walter had already pulled out his fiddle. Everyone backed up to clear a space for dancing as he started in with "Old Dan Tucker." Pa grabbed Mattie around the waist and swung her out. They were so handsome together, Pa with his broad shoulders and black hair with no gray in it at all, and beautiful Mattie, her pink face damp and flushed.

A trickle of sweat ran down under my arm. I had wanted to wear my best linsey-woolsey dress for the wedding, but I had forgotten how heavy it was, and the crowded room was stifling. I just had to get fresh air. Ma didn't want me wandering around the fort alone, but she was busy watching Addis dance with pretty Mrs. Holt. They were laughing and talking, and Addis was holding

Mrs. Holt much too close. With Ma's attention on them, it would be easy to slip away.

I stepped out of the building. Fort Boise was a small British Hudson's Bay Company trading post between the Snake and Boise rivers. The fort was only about a hundred feet square, its one story buildings arranged against twelve foot high adobe walls. There were the main building where Mattie had been married, a store, servants' dwellings, a kitchen, a milk house and an outdoor oven. The sudden burst of sun on the whitewashed buildings was blinding after the dark room, and I shaded my eyes against the glare. At least there was a little breeze. It helped, but still, the temperature must have been well over ninety. I knew there was a grove of willow trees west of the fort. I'd sit a while under their shade and cool off.

I swung across the dirt courtyard on my crutches. Indians, dressed in bright Hudson's Bay blankets, were busy trading and bargaining with the emigrants from our caravan. After months of venison jerky and beans and rice and potatoes, my mouth watered at the sight of their muskmelons, yellow squash, green beans and wild black-berries. Our squaw was selling goat's milk. I hadn't tasted milk since our two cows died last month, and I craved it. Sparky loved milk, too. If only I had a trinket or some fishhooks with me to trade, I'd buy a pitcherful.

I was looking so hard at a row of baskets heaped with shiny purple plums and dark huckleberries, I almost bumped into an Indian woman and a young Indian girl. They were standing by the open fort gate. I'd noticed them here yesterday in the same place. Both were barefoot and both wore makeshift flour sacking dresses. Now they were talking to young Mrs. Brown from our company.

Mrs. Brown was shaking her head. "No, we can't take your daughter with us in our wagon. We have so little food left and no room." Mrs. Brown rushed past me as if she were in a hurry to be gone.

That was strange. The odd-looking Indian woman must have

been asking Mrs. Brown to let her daughter travel in the Brown's wagon. It was hard not to stare at the Indian squaw. Her forehead slanted back from her nose almost to a point so she practically had no forehead at all. Holes had been pierced all around her earlobes where she must have once worn ornaments, and her arms and legs were tattooed with dark dotted lines. Then I realized she'd caught me staring at her.

"G-good morning," I stammered, embarrassed.

She smiled. "Good morning."

I smiled back at her. Then for lack of anything more to say, I smiled at her daughter.

The girl wasn't smiling at all. She was frowning so deeply, a scar over her eyebrow tightened into a ridge. But even frowning, she was pretty. She had a normal forehead, no tattooes, and no holes in her ears, either. She and I were about the same height. I was small for thirteen, but she looked my age, maybe even older. Her dark eyes seemed rounder and her cheeks narrower than most of the Indians I'd seen, and her chin was more pointed. She looked Indian, and yet somehow, not Indian.

"Ella Jane!"

It was Ma's voice. I turned around. Sure enough, Ma was hurrying across the courtyard toward us.

"Ella Jane, I told you not to wander around on your own," she scolded. "Now come back to . . ." Ma stopped short as she got a good look at the Indian woman and her daughter.

The Indian woman stepped forward and spoke right up. "Madame, I wish my daughter to go to the mission school at The Dalles. Can you take her there in your wagon?"

"Mission school?" Ma repeated in surprise.

"Oui, my child is to go to school there to become a Christian like me."

"You . . . you're a Christian?" Ma stammered just like I had.

"I was taught Christian ways at the Methodist mission. Now it is time for my child to be a Christian, too."

18

"But if you're not a heathen, then why is your . . . for what reason . . . is your . . ." Ma was stammering again.

The Indian woman waved her arm toward the Indian village on the bank of the Snake River. She didn't say anything for a minute as she waited for us to look around. Some of the Indian men lolled by their skin-covered tents. Other men were fishing, while still others were hanging their catch on huge wooden racks to dry. Squaws nursed their babies, or carried them on their backs as they cooked fish over their campfires. Naked children played under the cottonwood trees. Dogs and cats and tamed prairie wolves sniffed through rotting piles of fish heads and entrails, fighting over scraps.

The Indian woman turned back to us. "I am Chinook, not miserable Snake like these. It is Chinook way to shape the infant's head. My daughter Yvette's head is not shaped because as baptized Christians, her father and me would not permit it."

Yvette. What a beautiful name, not plain like Ella Jane. I looked at Yvette. Yes, she was beautiful, too. All of a sudden, I thought what fun it would be to have her travel with us. Since leaving Illinois, I'd had only one friend, Mary Herren, and now that Mattie was leaving our wagon, I knew I'd be especially lonely.

"Your husband is also a baptized Christian?" Ma straightened her shoulders with new purpose. Nothing was so important to Ma as the state of a Christian soul.

"Oui, my husband is Pierre Dumelle. We leave now for the north to trap. Yvette must study at the Christian mission until we return in the spring. Even now, with all my teaching, she prefers old Chinook ways."

I looked at Yvette again. So it was Yvette's French father who explained her round eyes and heart-shaped face. It made sense. I should have guessed her father wasn't Indian. This time Yvette returned my look. I had thought her eyes were dark brown, but now I saw yellow flecks of light in them. A sudden connection seemed to flash between us, though we spoke no words. Then the moment was over as Ma stepped between us to take the Indian woman's hand in hers. She was smiling one of her rare smiles, and her pale gray eyes fairly sparkled.

"I have supported church missionary work in the Oregon country for years. Now I have the opportunity to further it myself. My own daughter was just married, so we have space in our wagon for your child. We'll be leaving today at mid-afternoon, if that is agreeable with you."

Hurrah, Yvette was coming with us! We would have a wonderful time, I just know it. Yvette could teach me her language and I could teach her mine. I'd show her my books and embroidery, and we could play with Sparky together. Yes, even if Pa decided to take the cutoff, having Yvette with us would make all the difference.

Still Yvette didn't speak. Maybe her English wasn't very good, or maybe she was shy. It didn't matter. Traveling together, we'd soon get to know each other. I grinned at her to show her how pleased I was, but she didn't smile back. Instead, the thin scar over her eyebrow tightened into a narrow seam as she scowled down at her dusty bare feet.

CHAPTER THREE

WHAT A JOB IT WAS TO FORD THE Snake River. We were at it all afternoon. What took the most time was just waiting in line to cross over. When our turn finally came, Pa and Addis drove the teams into the river. Then they rode horseback all the way across beside the oxen to keep them going. Sometimes the Snake River was so high, the wagons had to be ferried to the other side, but the water was low enough this year for the teams to pull the wagons the whole way.

Though the river was low, it was wide, and Pa was especially careful to follow exactly where other wagons had already crossed safely before us. Pa kept the wagon bed pitched and calked to make it watertight, but our last few weeks of hot, dry weather had shrunk the wood. Ma, Yvette and I stuffed rags everywhere we thought water might leak in.

The three of us rode across the river in the wagon. We had to put the cover down so the wind wouldn't catch it and blow us around like a sailboat. With no protection, the sun blazed overhead like a fireball. The gnats and mosquitoes that swarmed all around us in great, black clouds added to our discomfort. Still, it was exciting. I rode backwards on my mattress as we made our bumpy way across the river so I wouldn't miss anything.

On the east bank, the wagons jostled each other for a place in line while the oxen bellowed and bawled their protest at being caught in the crush. A lot of the men were in the water on horseback, like Pa and Addis, whipping and yelling at their teams to keep them going. The commotion and noise had the dogs frantic. They barked and fought and chased each other up and down both sides of the river.

The livestock was crossing the water farther downstream and that was even worse confusion. Riders prodded the cattle into the river to swim across, but some of the stock was in such poor condition, they couldn't make it. I saw a couple of cows swept away by the current. Others drifted up against rocks, and the men had to use ropes to pull them back into the water.

Way over to one side, the fort Indians silently watched us. I wondered what they were thinking. Probably that we were all crazy. Maybe Yvette's mother was with them, come to see Yvette off. She'd be easy to spot among the Snakes in their bright Hudson's Bay robes. I shaded my eyes against the sun and searched the shoreline, but I didn't see her. She and Yvette must have said their good-byes earlier. For sure, Yvette wasn't looking back. She sat right up in front of the wagon, staring straight ahead. Her shoulders were squared, and her black braid looked like an exclamation line down her narrow back.

Everyone was too done in after crossing the river to go more than a couple of miles beyond it. We pulled into our wagon circle early for the night, which was fine with me. I didn't care if we ever got to the hot springs. That was where Pa had to make up his mind about the cutoff. At least he hadn't mentioned the cutoff since last night. Maybe after Mattie's wedding this morning, he'd decided us Thatchers had better stick together after all.

I was doubly glad to stop early. It would give Yvette and me more time to get to know each other. With Yvette walking and me riding in the wagon because of my leg, we hadn't even spoken. Once we had a chance to get together, I just knew we'd be friends.

We had a set night routine, and even the excitement of having Yvette with us didn't change it. As soon as we stopped, Pa unhitched the teams and led them out to graze. Addis hobbled our two horses, and let them loose inside the wagon circle for the night. After months of practice, the scouts had gotten so skillful at marking out a circling pattern for us, the last wagon in line always fit right in behind the first. It made a perfect corral for the horses. Ma sent Yvette out to gather kindling. I had my usual job of unpacking our cooking gear from the wagon. By the time Ma and I had supper started, Pa and Addis were back. Pa got to work setting up our tents just outside the wagon circle, while Addis built the campfires beyond the tents.

All the time I was working, I was hatching a plan in my mind. It was to be a surprise for Yvette. Ma was my only problem. I knew if I asked her permission, she'd say no. Then Ma herself solved everything.

"I'm going over to the Stocktons' wagon, Ella Jane. Mrs. Stockton isn't feeling well. Finish cooking supper and I'll be back soon. I want to eat early so we have time for our Bible lesson before dark."

What luck that Ma was famous for her doctoring. As soon as she'd left with her medicine case under her arm, I started in on the surprise. First I found our Turkey red tablecloth and napkins in the big leather trunk. Then I unlocked the false floor in the wagon and took out the spun brass candlesticks, good pewter plates and beautiful German silver Grandma Fleming had given us when we left Ohio. Just the sight of all Ma's best things set my heart to pounding. If only she didn't take a fit when she found out what I was up to.

I set up Ma and Pa's portable chairs and table as usual. Addis and I always ate on the ground off an India rubber cloth. I spread it out and covered it with the red tablecloth. Carefully, I laid Ma's silver, her pewter plates and her candlesticks set with two new candles on the cloth. Then I filled Pa's tin shaving mug with what wild flowers I could find, purple wild asters, Queen Anne's lace, and black-eyed Susans, and set them between the candlesticks. There, I was finished. Everything sparkled. The table really looked beautiful. When Yvette saw it, she'd know right away how special I thought she was, and how happy I was to have her with us.

Ma came back sooner than I expected. She took one look at my surprise, and her lips tightened into a thin line. "Oh, Ella Jane, what have you done?"

"Please, Ma, let it be, just for tonight. You use your best silver and plates for holidays, and having Yvette with us is a holiday, too. It's the Christian thing to do, Ma, really it is."

Ma sighed just to make sure I knew how displeased she was. "Well, all right, but only this once. And let me check everything over before you put them away again."

Out of the corner of my eye I saw Yvette coming toward us with the kindling. When Ma went over to show her where to store it under the wagon, I filled Yvette's plate with all the wonderful food Ma had bought at the fort before we'd left, a thick piece of juicy red salmon, fresh green beans, hot turnips mashed in goat's milk and a slice of sweet muskmelon. I didn't bother with the Indian camas cake. Yvette was probably tired of them. Instead, I heaped her bowl with salad greens and sprinkled them with precious oil and vinegar. Then I filled everyone else's plates and set them out, too.

As Pa passed me on the way to his table, he winked. "It looks like a celebration, Ellie Jay," he said.

I nodded, too excited even to answer. I looked around for Yvette. She stood by the rear wagon wheel, her head turned away from us.

"Suppertime," I called, trying not to sound too pleased with myself.

Ma and Pa had already pulled up their chairs to the table. Addis was seated cross-legged on the ground, ready to start. But Yvette didn't move.

"Yvette, we're waiting for you so we can ask the blessing." Ma's voice was crisp.

As Yvette started slowly toward us, I eased myself down to a sitting position, and laid my crutches behind me on the grass. I motioned for Yvette to sit down, too, but she just stood next to me, looking down at her place.

"We'll bow our heads in prayer," Ma said. Her grace was longer than usual, including as it did, guidance for the days ahead and right decisions. I knew Ma was praying for right decisions about the cutoff, but for once I didn't care about the cutoff. I only cared about Yvette, still standing beside me, her bare, brown feet set firmly in the thick grass.

. "Please sit down, Yvette," I said when Ma finished. Addis, who hadn't even noticed anything out of the ordinary, was already noisily eating.

Yvette stooped down, but instead of sitting, she picked up her pewter bowl and in one quick motion, emptied it over the grass in a spray of oil and vinegar and salad greens. It was such an astounding thing to do, even Addis stopped eating, his fork halfway to his mouth. Pa's back was to Yvette, so he didn't see her, but Ma did. The three of us stared as Yvette carefully wiped out the bowl with the hem of her dress as if the greens had been poisoned. Then she stepped over to the fire, picked up a brown camas cake from the frying pan, dropped it in her bowl, and walked back to the wagon. Leaning against the rear wheel, she picked up the camas cake in her fingers, and began to eat it.

I reached for my crutches to get up, to go over and explain to

Yvette that this was a party to welcome her, to show her how pleased we were she was with us. As I started to stand, Ma snapped her fingers to catch my attention. She gave a quick shake of her head as if to say, "No, leave her alone."

Ma was right. The way Yvette had refused to sit with us or eat anything but the camas cake, told us plainly enough that she wasn't interested in our food or my welcome either. Nothing I could say would make a difference. I sat down again, and without thinking, ate a forkful of mashed turnips. They were creamy and hot, but they tasted as dry as venison jerky in my mouth.

CHAPTER FOUR

"HOT SPRINGS! HOT SPRINGS AHEAD!"
Addis shouted as he rode down the line of wagons on his horse,
Major.

Addis is like Paul Revere, I thought, wiping my dirty face with
my handkerchief. I had been riding in the wagon all day, ever since
we broke camp west of the Snake River this morning. The wagon
cover was drawn tight against the west wind, for what little good
it did. I never saw such dust. Everything, including me, was covered
with it. Even my throat felt scratchy, and the closed wagon was
stifling hot.

All our different companies planned to meet at the hot springs
where we would rest for two days and get ready for the last leg

27

of the trip. And decide whether or not to take the cutoff. The last four hundred miles were supposed to be the hardest, but they couldn't be any worse than the ankle deep dust we'd struggled through all day. If the cutoff crossed country as barren dry as this, I didn't see how the wagons could ever make it.

As soon as we creaked to a stop, Ma was in the wagon. She wore one of Pa's broad-brimmed hats with a kerchief tied over her nose and mouth. When she pulled it down, I had to laugh. The bottom half of her face was white, and the top half was so dirty, she looked like a checkerboard.

"Thank the Lord we're out of that dust." She wiped her face like I had.

"Can we bathe right away?" I couldn't wait to soak my sore leg.

"Bathe, scrub, launder, rest. Two days isn't much for the teams to gather their strength, but it's better than nothing." Ma plucked a couple of dead leaves off her seedlings. She always kept her young apple and pear trees, her medicinal herb roots, and lilac and rose-bushes carefully damp. Like the livestock, they were watered first, no matter how scarce water was for the rest of us. Then she pulled the old quilt covering off her Liberty Chest and dusted the top with her apron. Ma's Liberty Chest traveled wherever she did. The handsome cherrywood chest had been built by her grandfather the year of American Independence, and Ma treasured it.

Pa stuck his head in the wagon. "Where's Addis? He hasn't unhitched the oxen and they're wild to get at the water."

"I haven't seen him since he rode by on Major," I answered.

"He's more'n likely over to Mrs. Holt's." Ma's voice was flat.

I was surprised. It was the first time Ma had mentioned Mrs. Holt outright. Pa looked startled, too, but he didn't say anything. He just dropped the wagon cover and disappeared.

Mrs. Holt was traveling alone, and there was lots of gossip about her. Maybe that's because she was so pretty. Some said she was a widow. Some said her husband had left her. Others claimed there had never been a husband at all. Mrs. Holt had started the trip with a young man she called Nephew. At Fort Bridger, Nephew had decided to turn back, leaving Mrs. Holt to struggle the rest of the way alone. Struggle wasn't exactly the word. Addis had made himself handy, milking her cow, repairing her wagon and harness, and setting up her camp each night. I wondered if Addis knew what had happened to Mr. Holt.

"That Addis," Ma grunted as she began to gather up everything in the wagon that wasn't tied down, and stuff it in a laundry sack. When she snatched Addis' jacket off the hook, I had the feeling she wished it were the scruff of Addis' neck. She threw a bar of soap in the sack and handed it to me.

"Be sure to scrub these good and clean, child," she said as she picked up the wooden wash tub, scrub board and her own sack of dirty laundry and left the wagon.

As soon as Ma was gone, I lifted the top of Sparky's bedroom tin. She was peacefully curled up in her nest of dry leaves and straw, fast asleep. Being a desert chipmunk, Sparky was probably the only one in the whole caravan who didn't mind the terrible heat and dust. For now I'd let her sleep, and she could exercise later.

What a relief to get out of the sweltering wagon. The air was hot all right, but at least we were camped in a beautiful green valley out of the dust. Tall ryegrass swayed in the breeze as far as the eye could see. A tree-lined river cut through the valley two hundred yards or so beyond our wagons. Between the river and our camp were the hot spring geysers, thin streams of water that gushed in the air, then fell back into ponds like a showering of raindrops. I felt better just seeing water and all that greenness.

Pa was unyoking the teams, with Addis nowhere in sight. As usual, Jackson and Ben, the lead yoke of oxen, patiently waited their turn to be unhitched. Rufus and Sock, always the loudest, bellowed to get at the water. When we had bought the oxen back in Missouri before starting out, their coats were shiny smooth and their velvet eyes were bright. Now they were rib-thin, with dull coats and even duller eyes. At least Pa spared them the whip, so they weren't scarred up like most of the teams.

I swung over to Pa on my crutches with my sack of laundry slung over my shoulder like St. Nicholas' pack. To my surprise, Yvette was standing with Pa. She must have been talking. At least Pa was nodding as if he were listening to her. Why, Yvette hadn't said a word since we started. I wasn't even sure she could talk. Now here she was, having a conversation with Pa.

"My Ellie Jay," Pa greeted me, using his special pet name for me. He reached out and rubbed my head the way he always did. Then he smiled at Yvette. Incredibly, she smiled back. If I had never heard her talk before, I most certainly had never seen her smile. She had straight white teeth with a chip off the corner of her front tooth that was somehow attractive. Her smile dimpled both her cheeks.

Pa dropped his hand to Yvette's shoulder. "I was just explaining about the cutoff. Yvette hadn't heard we were even considering it, but she tells me she knows this country well. She says we should take it, that it's shorter and easier than the regular route."

I could hardly believe my ears. Ever since last night, I'd avoided Yvette. Now here she was encouraging Pa to take the cutoff. I'd been so anxious to have Yvette come with us, and this was how she paid me back. Yvette smiled at me as if she expected me to smile, too. I was so stunned, all I could do was stare at her.

All of a sudden, Sock nudged me from the rear with his nose. I cried out in surprise. Pa threw back his head and laughed, and so did Yvette.

Impatiently, I straightened my laundry sack on my shoulder. "Well, there's some who've got work to do," I snapped. I heard a whine in my voice just like Mattie's, but I was too furious to care.

Women had already lined the banks of the hot spring ponds and started in on the scrubbing by the time I arrived. We'd been on the road over three months now, and this was only the third time we'd stopped long enough to do a thorough washing. Even so, the women seemed to be talking more than they were scrubbing. The younger children splashed each other in the warm water. My friend, Mary Herren, who was bathing her baby sister Bethie, waved me over to join her. I pretended not to see her. All I wanted to do right now was soak my leg. There was Ma. She was working beside a young woman who looked so much like my sister Lucy from the back, it startled me. The woman had fine golden hair that strayed from its knot just like Lucy's did, and she had the same frail look about her. Then she turned to speak to Ma, and I realized it was Mrs. Chambers who'd been traveling in our company the last few weeks.

I walked past everyone until I found a private spot under a slender willow tree. A flock of ducks swam away angrily quacking as I dropped my laundry sack and crutches on the ground and sank down by the pond's edge. I hiked up my skirts, unbuttoned my old cracked shoes and pulled off my stockings. I eased both legs into the warm water, stretched back and closed my eyes.

"Your leg is bad."

My eyes flew open. Yvette was hunkered down beside me. She was the one person in all the world I didn't want to see.

"Doctor Wilcox told me it will be fine," I said curtly.

"Non." Clear, final sounding.

My heart began to beat in a heavy rhythm. It was something I had tried not to think about. Still, there was that funny twisted look to it, and the pain that should have gone by now, five weeks after the accident. I glanced down at my leg. Even under water, I could see how much thinner my left leg was than my right.

Yvette was looking at my leg, too. "It needs care."

It was almost as if she were offering help. I didn't want it. I just wanted her to go away and leave me alone. But Yvette didn't move. She sat beside me looking out across the valley. As the silence stretched on, I studied the course of the rushing brown river that flowed beyond us. The water was only about ten feet wide, but it looked deep.

"I wonder what the name of that river is," I said, then could have kicked myself. I had no intention of getting into a conversation with Yvette.

"We shall follow its course for many miles."

Yvette meant on the cutoff. This river flowed from the west, and the cutoff headed west. Pa must have told Yvette he had decided for sure to take the cutoff. I sat right up.

"Did Pa tell you that?"

Yvette shook her head. "Non, I just know it."

She was right. I sensed it, too. Pa had made up his mind to follow Mr. Meek. "What is the name of the river?" I asked again.

Yvette watched the river for a moment, then turned and looked me right in the eye. "Malheur."

Malheur sounded French like everything else around here. "What does it mean?" I demanded, angry at Yvette, angry at Pa, angry at Mr. Meek, angry that we were to follow this muddy twisting river into the wilderness.

Though Yvette didn't drop her gaze from mine, she half closed her eyes so that her heavy eyelids looked like shutters being drawn. "Malheur means misfortune . . . ill luck . . ." she replied softly.

CHAPTER FIVE

I WAS RIGHT. PA HAD DECIDED TO TAKE the cutoff with Stephen Meek, and once Pa set his mind on something, he thought all the world should do the same. He spent most of the two days we were camped at the hot springs trying to convince everyone else to follow the cutoff, too. He liked to take Yvette with him, boasting, "This little girl knows the country like she'd lived here." I hardly saw Yvette for those two days and that suited me fine.

We'd hardly been roused by the reveille gun on the day we were to break camp, when Pa was up and at it again. By the time Ma and I started cooking breakfast, he'd already left for the Ingles' wagon.

33

"Why he feels he has to get everyone to follow that cutoff, I can't imagine," Ma grumbled, stirring the corn-meal mush harder than she had to. "I hate the thought of it. It's dangerous . . . dangerous . . ."

I thought so, too, but I couldn't admit it out loud. "Maybe it'll be all right, Ma," I said instead. "Mr. Hancock says if we follow the cutoff, we'll only meet harmless digger Indians and on the old route, the Walla Walla and Cayuse Indians can be dangerous. Then we'll meet Mattie and Henry at The Dalles and all raft down the Columbia River the rest of the way together."

Ma wasn't even listening. She was still muttering to herself. "Your father's so anxious to reach the promised land, but he's always the last to hitch up and get started. And with Addis on guard duty, he's got all the work to do alone." Ma suddenly seemed to realize I was standing beside her. "Fetch Yvette from the wagon and the two of you strike the tents, Ella Jane. I don't aim to eat dust all day. I'll go find your father and make sure he gets the teams hitched up in time for once. We can eat breakfast later." Ma pulled the pan of mush from the fire and hurried off.

The gray light of early dawn was washing the last of the stars from the sky as I headed for the wagon. The air was still cool and damp. A low mist hung over the Malheur River. Malheur . . . ill luck. Ma would say fretting about a name was silly superstition, but when my aching leg woke me at night, I couldn't help but think about it.

"Yvette?" I called, opening the wagon cover and climbing inside. Though a lard oil lamp was lit, it threw such a feeble light, I could hardly see. I heard a scratching that meant Sparky was awake. After breakfast, I'd clean out her cage and feed her the melon seeds I'd been saving.

In the dim light I saw Yvette standing in the middle of the wagon, dressed only in her thin cotton shift. "C'mon, Yvette, we have to . . ." I didn't finish. Now that my eyes were accustomed to

34

the dark, I saw that Yvette was standing in front of Ma's Liberty Chest with the top drawer open.

The wagon was only ten feet by four feet and packed so tight, there wasn't much room to move, but I reached Yvette in a second. I slammed the drawer shut. "Stay away from Ma's chest!"

Yvette backed up a step, her eyes wide with surprise.

"It's my mother's Liberty Chest. Her grandfather made it the year of American Independence. See, there's the date carved in the side, 1776. It's Ma's prized belonging and no one is ever allowed to touch it."

The chest was as much a part of Ma as her neatly knotted hair and gray eyes. She never moved anywhere without it. The only other furniture we'd brought were the two folding chairs, the table, a mattress and Ma and Pa's bedstead. *The Emigrant's Guide* had listed essentials to pack: guns, ammunition, clothing, bedding, tinware, cooking utensils, tents and tent poles, farm tools, spare oxen shoes, chains, strong ropes, crop seeds and seedlings, beads, tobacco and fishhooks for trading with the Indians. The rest of the space was taken up with staples and food. And Ma's Liberty Chest. In some ways it was an essential, too. Pa always complained about the room it took, but he knew Ma would never move without it.

"You'd better get dressed, Yvette, we've got work to do," I said.

Slowly, Yvette re-covered the Liberty Chest with the quilt. Then she laid her hand over the top, her fingers spread eagle. "To own another's prized belonging is to gain that person's power," she whispered.

"What do you mean?"

"It is nothing," Yvette replied, turning away from the chest. Then she shrugged her shoulders. "I am not dressed because I cannot find my clothing."

I'd forgotten. Ma had washed Yvette's flour sacking dress last night, but it was so frayed and thin, it had torn to shreds. "Your dress fell apart when Ma washed it. You can wear my blue calico dress hanging there on the hook. It should fit pretty well."

"Non. I want my own dress."

In a rush of understanding, I knew how Yvette felt. In my whole life, I had only owned one dress that wasn't a hand-me-down from Lucy or Mattie or cut down from one of Ma's. I loved that dress so much, I had worn it until I couldn't stuff myself into it any more.

"Maybe you can wear something of your own." I nodded toward the woven grass basket Yvette had brought with her.

Yvette shook her head and stepped in front of the basket as if to guard it. For the first time I wondered what was in it. Though it was only the size of a hatbox, it probably held everything Yvette owned in the world.

"You can wear my best red dress if you want," I offered.

Yvette shook her head again. She had the same, wild frightened look Sparky had when Pa first caught her. I didn't blame Sparky then, and I didn't blame Yvette now. All of a sudden, I realized how much I would hate to be in her place, traveling with strangers to an unknown school, eating a different kind of food, not even wearing her own clothes. Smiling encouragement, I took my dress off the hook and held it out to her.

My smile seemed to help. Yvette's expression softened and the pinched look around her mouth eased. She looked at my dress a moment, then took it from me. Slowly, she stepped into it, putting her arms through the sleeves. It was so short her brown legs and bare feet stuck out awkwardly. She'd put it on backwards, too, but I'd have cut out my tongue before I told her. As she started to button it up, slipping half the buttons in the wrong buttonholes, I decided I'd better leave her to struggle with it alone.

As I climbed out of the wagon, I saw the sky had already turned from gray to dusty blue and the sun was higher, breaking the cool dawn like an oven door being cracked open. The grasshoppers and crickets were going at it like a thousand fiddles. It would be another hot day.

Camp was bedlam. Almost everyone had finished breakfast and was well under way with preparations to leave. Some had already struck their tents and herded their oxen into the wagon circle to yoke them. I didn't see Pa anywhere, or Ma either. We'd never get off. The feeling of panic I'd tried to keep down for two days began to rise in my chest. We couldn't be last in line today. We just couldn't. Not starting on the cutoff. No, from now on, I wanted to be right up front, the first in line, instead of straggling along at the end the way we usually did.

"Is this the Thatcher wagon?"

I hadn't even noticed the man standing by our campfire until he waved me over. He was a tall, rawboned man with bowed legs, long tangled hair and skin like polished leather. It was Stephen Meek. He tipped his dirty, beaver-trimmed white hat.

"Is your father about?" He had a soft, slurred accent, and I wondered if he was from the South.

"No, he's out rounding up the teams." Mr. Meek's back was to our wagon, so he didn't see Yvette climb down and start toward us as I did. Then she hesitated, studied Mr. Meek for a moment, then scooted behind the rear wagon wheel.

"You must be Thatcher's daughter," Mr. Meek was saying.

I nodded. Mr. Meek was an old-time mountaineer and he looked it. He wore a loose coat of antelope skins trimmed with beaver, and fringed buffalo leggings that were so tight, I wondered how he could sit on a horse. His shoulder strap held his powder horn and bullet pouch. A big pistol was jammed in his belt, and his moccasins sported iron Mexican spurs that must have been ten inches long. I liked him even less close up than I did from a distance.

Mr. Meek didn't seem to notice my disapproval. "I come to thank your father for persuadin' some of the party to take the cutoff," he said. "I'll be pilotin' about two hundred wagons, nearly a thousand emigrants, and all their livestock."

It was unbelievable that a thousand people, including us

Thatchers, were trusting their lives to this one unsavory looking man!

"Wal, again, my thanks to your father when he returns." Mr. Meek turned to go, then stopped. He had seen Yvette. He quickly strode over to where she stood behind the wagon wheel.

"Who's this?" he yelled back to me.

As I headed toward them on my crutches, Mr. Meek took Yvette's arm and pulled her out from behind the wheel.

"Yvette is traveling with us. We're taking her to The Dalles," I answered, not that it was any of Mr. Meek's business.

"So you're the girl I heard talk about who's supposed to know the country." Mr. Meek took Yvette's chin and yanked her face into the light. "What's your last name?"

Yvette's jaw tightened, but she didn't answer.

"Your name!"

"Dumelle."

"By God, I thought I recognized you. You're Dumelle's brat with a Chinook mother, ain't that so?"

How dare Mr. Meek speak to Yvette like that when she was a guest in our wagon? Before I had a chance to protest, Mr. Meek released Yvette's chin with a jerk and turned to me.

"A craftier Indian than a Chinook never been born. They ruled the whole lower Columbia with their tradin' and sellin', and the richest of 'em all was this one's old grandfather. He must be near a hundret by now. As for Dumelle, he's nothin' but a wretched cur. No, the offspring of a Chinook and a Dumelle is trouble. I won't have her traveling with us. Tell your father to get rid of her."

Mr. Meek's face was brick-red with anger. He slapped his big hat on his head and stomped away, the rowels on his spurs jangling.

I was furious at myself. I should have stood up to him. Ma would have. Instead, the anger just boiled inside me ready to explode. Mr. Meek wanted us to throw Yvette away like her old flour sack dress. Well, we wouldn't do it.

I looked at Yvette. If I was expecting to see tears, I was wrong. She was even angrier than I was. Her eyes shone with deep yellow lights, and as her gaze met mine, I felt that same sudden charge of sympathy flash between us that I had felt the first day we met at Fort Boise.

$\mathbf{M}$A RETURNED TO THE WAGON FIRST.
She must have found Pa. He came right after her, leading the oxen.
We all ate a quick breakfast standing up. The way Ma rushed us
through the meal, she didn't give me a chance to mention Mr.
Meek's visit or his message.

"You girls wash these up while I pack the wagon." Ma handed
Yvette the crate of dirty cooking utensils.

Yvette didn't speak until we reached the banks of the hot springs
pond. A whole flock of ducks noisily flapped away at our approach,
and I wondered if they were the same ducks I'd disturbed the other
day. Yvette waved me aside as she stooped down and started
scrubbing.

"I will do these," she offered.

That was all right with me. It was hard for me to kneel. I propped myself against a willow tree and dried the dishes as Yvette washed them. We were sitting just where we'd sat two days ago when we had talked about the Malheur River. I remembered how angry I'd been at Yvette that day for urging Pa to take the cutoff. Looking back on it now, I realized she had only meant to be helpful. There was no way she could have known how strong I felt against it.

"About that Meek man . . ." Yvette said hesitantly, as if the words were hard to get out.

I laughed. "Don't worry that I'll say anything. If Mr. Meek has a message for Pa, he can deliver it himself."

Yvette smiled so that her dimples grooved her cheeks. Then she unexpectedly laughed. It was a lovely, tinkling sound that reminded me of the bells Pa used to hang on our newborn lambs.

"It is important for me to continue this journey." Yvette was suddenly serious. She studied my face for a moment as if she were trying to make up her mind about me.

I was suddenly serious, too. Something had happened between Yvette and me, and though I couldn't describe it, I knew the bad feeling between us was gone. It wasn't as if we were friends yet, but the possibility was at least there, and I felt good about it.

Yvette scoured the last of the pots and handed it to me to dry. When I was finished, I picked up my crutches to leave, but Yvette held out her hand to stop me. "Sit," she ordered.

She lifted the skirt of her blue calico dress. She was wearing it frontwards now, and Ma had showed her how to button it, but she still looked uncomfortable in it. A worn deerskin pouch hung around her waist. She pulled open the bag, dipped in her fingers and scooped out some fishy smelling ointment. She leaned over my left leg, spread the grease the length of it and began to rub. As she worked in the ointment, she gently bent my leg back and forth at the knee.

At first it hurt, but then gradually the pain lessened. As Yvette worked, she hummed a kind of tuneless chant under her breath. I closed my eyes, and my mind drifted. I didn't think about my leg, or the cutoff, or Mr. Meek or anything.

"We must return now."

Yvette was finished. I opened my eyes, feeling so sleepy and comfortable, I had no idea how much time had passed. Yvette had put away her deerskin pouch, and was packing up the last of the cooking gear. She lifted up the crate and started back toward camp.

It was time to go. I got to my feet, braced myself on my crutches and started after her. I tried to keep up, but Yvette walked so fast she had already disappeared around the side of the wagon by the time I reached the outskirts of camp.

"Ella Jane!"

It was a wonderfully familiar voice. When I turned around, I saw Mattie running toward me. We met in a big bear hug.

"Oh, Mattie, I'm so happy to see you." I looked her up and down. It had only been four days since the wedding. Did she look older, wiser, more beautiful?

Mattie straightened her dress as if my hug had mussed her all up. "Where's Ma, Ella Jane? I'm so upset, I just got to talk to her."

It was the same old Mattie after all. I wondered if she still tried to hide her whine from Henry. "Ma's in the wagon packing to leave. What's wrong?" I asked as we started toward camp together.

"As soon as Henry and I arrived last night, we heard about all the people following that dreadful Mr. Meek, and we heard that Pa aims to go, too. Tell me it isn't true."

"I guess maybe it is . . ." Even now, when we were almost ready to leave, it was hard to talk about the cutoff.

Mattie stopped and glared at me as if it were my fault. "What is Pa thinking of? Anything could happen, like sickness or another accident like you had. Why, the whole caravan could get lost."

Mattie was voicing all the fears I'd imagined myself, and I'd

42

guessed right. Hearing them out loud made them seem worse. A thick rush of blood raced to my head and I felt dizzy.

"If Pa's so anxious to take the cutoff, let him and Addis go. You and Ma come with Henry and me in the Jenkins' wagon."

What a wonderful idea. I should have thought of it myself. Then I remembered Yvette. There wouldn't be room for her, too. Besides, knowing the Jenkins, I was sure she wouldn't be welcome. And it wouldn't be proper for her to travel alone with Pa and Addis.

"I guess it wouldn't work out, Mattie, but thanks anyway," I said. "C'mon, let's surprise Ma."

Mattie shook her head. "No, I want to see Ma alone. I got private matters to talk over with her."

I watched Mattie climb in the wagon. I just bet she was going to have a married-woman talk with Ma, and I wished I could listen. Instead, I scattered the last of the campfire ashes with the tip of my crutch. Pa was busy greasing the wagon wheel hubs, for what little good it did. They always squeaked and groaned no matter how much he tarred them. Even now, some of the other wagons were lined up waiting for the starting trumpet. That meant it must be close to seven o'clock. It felt hotter than seven, with the west wind already swirling little flurries of dust and trash around the camp. The constant west wind never ceased. It seemed as if we'd been traveling into its hot breath forever.

Mattie came rushing out of the wagon in tears. She gave me a quick kiss, hugged Pa, then flew down the line of wagons away from us. In her haste, her poke bonnet slipped off so that it flapped against her back as she ran. Her blonde curls bounced. I watched until she was out of sight. I didn't dare let myself think when we would see Mattie again, *if* we saw her again. That was ridiculous. We'd all be meeting at The Dalles before we knew it, and traveling the rest of the way to the Willamette Valley together.

Pa had finished greasing the wheels and hung the leather tar bucket back on the rear axletree of the wagon. He led his horse Campbell over to Ma and helped her mount. Even Yvette sensed we were ready to move out. She took a position next to the rear left wheel as Pa pulled his rawhide whip from its holder and stepped to the left of Jackson and Ben.

"In the wagon, Ella Jane, and be fast about it," Ma called.

I'd put it off as long as I could. I took one last look around camp as I climbed in the wagon. The men were hurriedly making last-minute adjustments to teams and harnesses. Children and dogs raced wildly around. One team of oxen loudly refused to be yoked. A riderless horse galloped pell-mell through camp. Though it still looked like bedlam, I knew it wasn't. We'd been on the road since May, and now, at the end of August, everyone knew exactly what he was doing. When that cow horn trumpet sounded, every wagon would fall into place like an army on the march.

As I settled down on my mattress and stretched out, I suddenly realized my leg didn't hurt as much as usual. Even though I'd had more than two days' rest without the awful jarring of the wagon, I wondered if Yvette's ointment and exercise hadn't helped, too. Maybe she would work on it again sometime.

I reached up for Sparky's cage. Sparky gnawed through anything made of wood, so building her cage had been a problem. Pa had finally lashed two tobacco tins together, cut holes for doors, and air holes in the tight fitting lids. One tin served as her bedroom and the other as her storeroom. Since Sparky's exercise cage was just a big overturned basket with a floor, I always watched her when she was in it to keep her from gnawing.

"Tsst. Tsst. Tsst." I dropped the melon seeds I'd saved in my apron pocket. I did my best to ignore what was going on outside, but that was hard. The shouting and cursing and animal noises were at their loudest. As usual, Mrs. Hall was yelling for her four-year-old son. James Hall always seemed to disappear at the critical starting moment.

Sparky must have been hungry. She scurried out of her cage, across my lap, and disappeared into my pocket, with only her long straight tail sticking out. I emptied out the dirty straw from her sleeping tin and replaced it with new straw from my mattress. As I scooped Sparky out of my pocket and slipped her into the exercise cage, I was aware of the sudden quiet. Only the nicker of a horse and the lowing of an ox broke the stillness. I knew what that silence meant. It was always like that before we started.

"Ta-ta-ta-de-ta," blew the trumpet.

"Turn out! Turn out!" came the cry.

It was the signal to start.

Swish. Pa's twenty foot long bullwhip sang through the air. All around I heard whips snap and the men urging on their teams. I braced myself on the sides of the mattress as every muscle in my body protested. I squeezed my eyes shut. Our wagon gave a lurch. The wheels creaked as we began to move. It was really happening. We were headed west on the cutoff. I put my arm around Sparky's cage as if to protect her, then threw myself down on the mattress, burying my head in my pillow.

CHAPTER SEVEN

Now that we were on the cut-off, two things were uppermost in my mind. One, that we find plenty of water, grass and wood each night, and two, that we keep moving. So far, so good. For two days, ever since leaving the hot springs, we had followed the course of the Malheur River, and Mr. Meek had found us good camping sites both nights. And we'd kept moving, if what we did could be called moving. It was one of the worst stretches of road we'd hit yet. The whole barren countryside was covered with such sharp rocks, it was a wonder our wagons didn't shake to pieces.

On the second day out, we traveled a good distance, twelve miles. That night we stopped in a narrow valley where alder, cottonwood and willow trees bordered a sinking rivulet, with enough water and timber to satisfy even me. As soon as we had circled for night camp, I was out of the wagon. Every bone in my body ached from the hard day's ride. Even my head hurt.

Ma and Pa were already seeing to the teams. If the bad road was hard on me, it was torture on the oxen. Their feet were cut and bleeding. As I stretched to get the kinks out of my shoulders and back, I watched Ma and Pa work on poor Sock. He lowed with pain and fear. First they scrubbed his hooves, then while Ma tried to quiet him, Pa scraped away all the festered raw flesh. When that was done, he poured on boiling tar to seal the wound. It was a messy job, and painful for Sock, too, but we had to keep the teams going. We had counted on yoking up a milk cow if an ox gave out, but both our cows had bloated and died last month after drinking alkali water.

I waited until Ma and Pa had finished with Sock, but hadn't yet started on Rufus. "Ma, can I talk to you?"

She nodded without looking up.

"Can I sleep outside in the tent tonight? I can't bear that wagon another minute."

"I guess so. Make sure you have plenty of blankets. The night air is cold."

Ma still hadn't looked up, but Pa did. He reached over and rubbed my head. "It's been a hard trip for you, hasn't it, Ellie Jay, harder on you than anyone."

Pa was always so understanding. I wasn't surprised to see him blink his eyes as if tears were just beneath the surface.

"I'm just sore from today's ride, Pa, that's all. I'll be fine."

"It's been hard on all of us," Ma retorted. "Giving up our family and farm was bad enough, but to follow this wretched road to nowhere is sheer folly."

Pa raised his eyebrows at me as if to say, "Complaints, complaints." The funny thing was that Pa understood me, but he didn't understand Ma at all. I did. I knew just what she meant. Every time

I thought about Lucy or Benton or Grandma Fleming, I felt awful, too. And I knew Ma worried about Lucy's poor health. She said special prayers for Lucy every night.

I had a double reason for asking to sleep in the tent. I wanted to get out of the wagon, but I wanted to see more of Yvette, too. After our closeness that day at the hot springs, we'd hardly exchanged ten words. Maybe that was because Ma and Pa were always around, and Yvette never talked much in front of them. Being alone with Yvette in the tent would give us a chance to get to know each other better.

Neither of us spoke as we set up our tent that night. It was hardly more than a canvas sheet hung between poles, so it didn't take long. Though we didn't talk, it didn't really matter. The silence between us was comfortable.

Ma was right about it being cold. The thin mountain air was oven-hot in the daytime, but dropped to near-freezing at night, and now that it was almost September, the days were getting shorter. Shivering, I laid my India rubber cloth on the ground, spread my blanket roll on top of it, and was about to crawl in when Yvette stopped me.

"Let me see your leg," she said.

I nodded. In the back of my mind, I had been waiting for Yvette to speak first. I wrapped up in my blanket, pulled my nightdress above my knee and laid my leg in Yvette's lap. As Yvette started to rub it with her ointment, I smelled the same fishy odor I'd smelled the day at the hot springs pond. While Yvette exercised my leg gently back and forth, she hummed her tuneless chant. As my stiff muscles began to loosen, I gazed up at the sky. The stars shone like a million tapers, and the familiar bright constellations jumped out at me from the huge blackness.

"Look at the Great Dipper and the Little Dipper, Yvette." I pointed them out to her.

"Ah, non, those are not their names. Now that night has come, I can tell the true tale of how those stars came to be."

48

Though Yvette spoke in a lovely, lilting voice that reminded me of her tinkling laugh, she sounded distant, as if she were addressing a great gathering, instead of just me.

"In the land north of this place, on the coast," she began, "the people did not like the height of the sky. It was too low. Sometimes, when they climbed into the big cedars, they disappeared into the sky world and never returned. The wise men met to decide what to do.

" 'If all our tribes work together, we can push the sky higher up,' said one of the wise ones.

" 'We must cut many long poles so everyone can push on the sky together,' said a Chinook chief.

" 'Shall we meet one moon from now, as the sun comes up?' asked another chief.

" 'Good!' agreed the members of the Council. 'Let all our tribes shout YA-HOO as they push. In our many languages, that will mean, "Raise all together." '

"When the sky-raising day came, the earth shook with the loud YA-HOO. All the people pushed as hard as they shouted. Their mighty efforts lifted the sky.

"But a few hunters who had been away from home did not know of the sky raising. Three hunters and their dog had chased four great elk up a mountain where the earth and sky nearly met. The elk leaped into the sky world and the hunters and their dog jumped after them. When the sky was raised, the hunters and the elk were raised with it. They were turned into stars and can still be seen in the sky world. But the people on earth were happier, and the sky has remained high overhead ever since.

"See the hunters and the elk?" Yvette pointed to the sky, and there they were. The three hunters and their tiny dog were the handle of the Great Dipper and the four elk were the bowl.

"Now it is time for sleep." Yvette swung my leg off her lap and lay down on her woven cattail mat. She pulled her handsome, thick sea otter robe up over her.

I snuggled into my scratchy blanket roll. My leg felt better than it had since I hurt it, and I knew I'd sleep well for once. Dimly I was aware of Ma and Pa settling down in their tent next to ours, and the camp noises quieting for the night. I must have fallen right asleep.

Suddenly I was awake, my heart pounding. I sat straight up. Yvette was awake, too, and sitting up like I was. Then I heard the sound that had awakened me. It was a coyote. He was far away, but his howl carried clearly in the thin air. I couldn't really call it howling. It was more of a singing, rising and falling, like a human voice. I'd heard that same eerie cry somewhere before. Of course. It was at Fort Boise, the night before Mattie's wedding, the night before Yvette had joined us.

"Do you hear that?" I whispered to Yvette, anxious for the sound of her voice.

As Yvette turned toward me, the bright moon lit up her face. It shone with excitement, and her dark eyes glowed like an animal's in the dark.

"Wh-what is it?" I stammered.

I could see Yvette's lips turn up in a private kind of smile. "It is Stankiya. He follows me as I hoped."

"Stankiya?"

"My guardian spirit. He calls me with his spirit-power song."

"Guardian spirit?" I was beginning to sound like an echo.

Yvette put her hand up for silence. The strange song was farther away now, but we could still hear it. A shudder skittered up my back, just as it had the first time I'd heard that forlorn cry. "What do you mean, your guardian spirit?" I asked again.

"Stankiya will guide me on my vision quest. I shall do what he tells me. After that, I shall be a new person, with a new name. To others I will seem the same. Inside, I shall be changed forever."

"You mean right now?"

"Non. I must fast and rest the day before and the day after my quest. Stankiya will tell me when."

"I don't understand. What will you have to do?"

Yvette held up her hand again. I strained to pick up the distant coyote song, but all I heard was the colicky Herren baby crying and one of the guards softly playing a mouth organ.

"He is gone, but it does not matter. He will return." Yvette dropped her hand and lay down again. In minutes her even breathing told me she was asleep.

Sleep was the furthest thing from my mind. What a strange night. Maybe it was all a dream. No, my leg really did feel better, and there, high in the sky world, twinkled the hunters and the elk. And I knew I had heard that coyote. I shivered and pulled my blankets up around my ears. I saw my breath in the cold air, but I was shivering from more than the cold. Tonight I'd seen a side of Yvette no one else even knew existed. It was our secret. I was sure that tomorrow she would be as silent and withdrawn as ever. Even so, Yvette had only revealed to me what she wanted to, a fraction of what she was really all about, and I couldn't help but wonder about the rest.

CHAPTER EIGHT

THE NEXT DAY THE ROAD SEEMED
rougher than ever. The wagon bounced so hard over the rocky
terrain, I had to clench my jaws to keep my teeth from chattering.
Tremendous canyons and high rimrock ridges loomed to the north
and south of us. We traveled slower and slower as the road became
narrower and steeper. At least we were still moving.

I made myself keep busy all morning so as not to panic. I had
saved the last of the melon seeds to bribe Sparky into learning to
sit up and beg on command. But she ignored me and spent the
morning running around her exercise cage. Then I worked on my
sampler, but the road was so bumpy, my stitches came out even

more crooked than usual. Though I tried to read, I couldn't keep my mind on that either.

As soon as we stopped for our nooning break, I was out of the wagon. Pa and Addis were already checking over the oxen. The animals stood with bowed heads as if they didn't have the strength to lift them. Their feet were covered with blood. Pa looked terribly worried as he ran his hand over Jackson's right foreleg. I watched a few minutes, waiting for a chance to talk to Pa. I needed his assurance that the road wasn't so bad after all, that it would get better soon, but he was too busy to notice me.

I'd find Ma. She'd tell me. She was just climbing out of the wagon carrying her medicine case. As soon as she saw me, she hurried over.

"We'll eat later, Ella Jane. Sarah Chambers has taken sick and her husband's asked me to look in on her. She's such a frail little thing, I hope it's not serious."

"The road's going to get easier, isn't it, Ma, just as soon as we're through these mountains?"

Ma shrugged. "Who's to say. Your father's the expert on this cutoff, not me."

Yvette knew this country. She'd tell me the road would improve soon, that this was just the worst of it. "Where's Yvette?" I asked Ma.

"I sent her to the creek to pick currants for a pie. If you go, don't cross over the creek, Ella Jane." Ma's expression was as worried as Pa's, but I had the feeling she was worried about Mrs. Chambers, not about the road, the oxen or me. She tucked her medicine case under her arm and walked quickly away.

As soon as she was gone, I took one of the blue water buckets from its hook on the side of the wagon. I wondered what Yvette would be like when we were alone. She had been her same stand-offish self in front of Ma and Pa this morning, just as I had guessed she would be. She'd acted as if last night had never happened, but I knew differently. I remembered everything she had said, and I remembered that coyote. My leg knew differently, too. It felt stronger this morning.

I got a firm grip on my crutches and made my way past the teams. Pa looked up. "Where are you going, Ellie Jay?"

"Down to the creek to pick currants with Yvette."

Pa's face was serious. "Those canyons come down mighty close to the water. That's panther and wildcat country. Rattlesnakes, too. Stay in sight of the wagons, hear, and don't cross over the creek."

Addis grinned. "Yeah, you're so puny, a panther might mistake you for a juicy nooning morsel."

"All right, enough of that, Addis," Pa scolded, but he was grinning, too.

I stomped off without saying good-bye. It was fine for Pa and Addis to joke. Neither of them was the runt of the family like me.

It was a hot day, but a cool breeze made it bearable. The late summer sky was a robin's egg blue dotted with cottony white clouds. Fresh willows and alders bordered the creek. The willows' yellow-green leaves fluttered in the breeze so that the whole grove of trees seemed to be dancing. Low, full currant shrubs grew by the water, clustered with fat, red berries. I dropped a few in my bucket, then looked around for Yvette.

Downstream, the men were driving the first of the cow column to the water, struggling to control the thirsty cattle. Upstream, a couple of big boys were filling their water kegs. I didn't see Yvette anywhere.

Then something blue across the creek caught my attention. It was my blue calico dress. Yvette was on the other side of the creek. She was flattened behind a pine tree, peering around it as if she were watching something. After a moment, she half-slid, half-scurried twenty feet or so to the protection of the next tree. She was only about fifty feet away from the rimrock ledges of the canyons. Pa had said those canyons were full of panthers and wildcats.

"Yvette, come back!" I shouted.

She heard me, but instead of turning back, she waved furiously

54

at me to be quiet. Then she darted out from behind the tree and ran right toward the canyon. I had never seen anyone run so fast. Only the tips of her bare toes touched the ground as her long strides covered the distance in a flash.

She probably didn't know how dangerous those canyons were. I had to stop her. I waded into the shallow creek, but the rocky bottom was uneven, and my berry bucket was awkward to carry. Halfway across, one of my crutches slipped out from under me and I caught myself just in time. I had to get rid of my bucket. I heaved it with all my might to the far bank where it rolled over and over, scattering the few currants I had already picked. Without the bucket, I forded the creek easily.

Yvette had already reached the outcroppings of rock that led into the canyon. Then she was out of sight. A big turkey buzzard circled overhead, then winged down, landing with outstretched claws on the branch of a stunted pine tree. With his red, wrinkled bare head and wings folded around his hunched-up body, he was disgusting looking.

"Yvette, come back!" I called again.

I started toward the canyon, trying not to look at the buzzard or think about the rattlesnakes that were sure to be resting in the shade of the rocks. I walked slower and slower as I approached the place where Yvette had disappeared. I was surrounded by an immense silence. The shriek of a distant animal echoed through the canyon walls, as a dry little lizard darted across my path.

"Leave us alone."

I jumped at the sound of Yvette's voice behind me, but when I turned around I didn't see her. Then I looked up. She stood on a ledge eight or nine feet above the ground, braced against a pine tree that grew out of the shaly rock.

"I was following Stankiya. You frightened him and he fled." Yvette's angry voice was low, but it carried as if she had been standing beside me.

Stankiya. That was the name of her guardian spirit, the coyote that had been calling to her last night. I felt my cheeks flush. "I . . . I only wanted to warn you about the panthers and snakes . . ."

"That is my concern, not yours." Yvette scowled down at me, the line of her scar tightening over her eye. Last night Yvette had soothed my leg and talked to me as a friend. Now she was as cold and gruff as if we were enemies.

"I . . . I'm sorry, Yvette . . ."

POOOWWW!

The crack of a rifle boomed down by the creek, bouncing back and forth between the canyon walls.

"Ella Jane!"

It was Pa. He was looking for me. And I had crossed the creek after both he and Ma had forbidden it. Panic stricken, I looked up at Yvette as if she could tell me what to do. But she only pointed to herself and shook her head.

"I was not here," she mouthed the words. Then she quickly worked her way around the corner of the ledge where she'd been standing. In a moment, she was out of sight. All was silence again. The turkey buzzard had long since taken flight. His dark feathers shone almost purple as he winged higher and higher.

"Ella Jane!" Pa's voice was closer.

I had to answer. "Here I am, Pa."

I needed a reason for being here. Frantically, I looked around. The ground was dotted with brown pine cones. I dropped my crutches and threw as many cones into my apron as I could.

Pa reached me first, with Addis right behind him. They were both breathless from running. "Ellie Jay, I thought you were lost . . ." Pa couldn't finish. He reached out and hugged me so tight, the pine cones spilled from my apron. His heart was pounding under his damp, rough shirt and I knew mine was pounding, too.

"You little goose," Addis yelled. "These canyons are crawling with snakes. It was just lucky I went to the creek for water and saw your blue bucket on the far side."

Pa dropped his arms from around me. "I thought I told you not to cross the creek."

I stooped to pick up the scattered pine cones. "I'm sorry I upset you, Pa, but I wanted to gather these cones for Sparky. She loves the seeds."

"How dare you disobey me? Where's Yvette?"

Yvette had asked me not to tell on her. If Pa knew she was here, he might press her with questions she didn't want to answer, and after all, Stankiya was a secret between Yvette and me. Still, in my heart, I knew it was more than that. If I told Pa that Yvette was hiding, she would be angry, and Yvette's anger frightened me.

"Yvette? Ah, no . . . ah, I crossed the creek on my own. Yvette is picking berries upstream." I knew my cheeks were burning, but I forced myself to look Pa square in the face.

"We'll talk about this back at camp."

What a relief. Pa seemed to accept my lie. He picked up my crutches and handed them to me. Just as I was fixing them under my arms, a sudden flurry of dust and rocks showered down from the ledge behind us. I froze. The little landslide came from the very place where Yvette was hiding. The shaly rock must have given way under her feet.

Pa put his finger to his lips for silence. Quickly he loaded his rifle and pulled back the hammer. He tiptoed over to the ledge and flattened himself against it. I stared in horror. Pa thought some kind of animal was up there. If he took aim and shot, he might kill Yvette.

"Wait, Pa," I cried out. "It's Yvette hiding on the ledge."

Pa stopped as suddenly as if I'd fired a gun myself. He stared at me, his face blank with surprise. Then he stepped out into the open and walked around to the far side of the ledge where he could get a good view. He looked up. I could tell by his expression that he saw Yvette, but he didn't speak to her, and she didn't come out of hiding. He walked back to where I stood watching.

"I can't fault the Indian girl, Ella Jane, perhaps she's never been taught. But you have, and your lying to me is unforgivable."

Pa turned around and walked away. His shoulders sagged and his footstep was heavy. Addis glared at me, then hurried after Pa. I had never lied to Pa before, not ever, and the disappointment on his face was almost more than I could bear.

CHAPTER NINE

INSTEAD OF THE ROAD GETTING BETTER
over the next three days, it got worse. The higher we traveled
into rimrock country, the rockier the road became. It was as if in
some ancient time, the heavens had opened up and hailed down
a storm of sharp, black stones. There was no relief from them.
During those three days we only traveled twenty-four miles, far
less than the twelve miles a day we had averaged since starting
out in Missouri.

Wagons broke. Oxen gave out. I cringed every time I heard a
rifle shot. When an ox caved in, he just lay down and wouldn't
get up. His owner had to either leave him there to die, or shoot

him so he wouldn't suffer. I couldn't bear to think of our oxen giving out. They had become as dear to us as family pets.

I fretted over our slow progress, but in one way, I was glad for the bad road. It kept Pa too busy to pay attention to me. For three days now, he had scarcely looked my way, let alone talked to me. For sure he hadn't rubbed my head or called me Ellie Jay in his teasing voice. At least he hadn't told Ma about my lie, or I knew I'd have heard plenty from her.

On the third day of hard travel, we circled earlier than usual for the night. Almost all our wagons needed repairs. The oxen, the horses, the livestock and people, too, were exhausted. We had scarcely stopped before Ma was in the wagon, rummaging through the top drawer of her Liberty Chest where I knew she kept her medicines and herbs.

"Start supper, Ella Jane. I'm going to Sarah Chambers' wagon. Her fever is worse."

Ma didn't wait for my reply. Maybe it was just as well she was so worried about Mrs. Chambers. She hadn't even noticed how angry Pa was at me. When she was gone, I got out the crate of cooking gear and pushed it across the wagon floor. A week ago, I wouldn't have been able to do that, but my leg was stronger now. Yvette had been working on it every night, almost as if she wanted to make up for me being in trouble. Sometimes she told an Indian tale as she exercised and rubbed my leg with ointment, and sometimes she just hummed her tuneless chant. Though we never talked about it, I was sure every night we both listened for Stankiya as well. I know I did. We heard plenty of coyote conversations, all right, but never that strange singing call that sent shivers up my back.

The wagon cover opened again. This time it was Addis. He hurried to the back of the wagon where he kept his belongings, and started to brush out his tangled red hair in front of the looking glass.

"Addis, take out the cooking gear box for me, will you please?" I asked.

"If I have time."

"Where are you going? You have to unhitch the teams." Today was Pa's turn on guard duty and Addis was responsible for the oxen.

"I'll be back in a while." Addis picked up the crate of cooking gear, and carried it out of the wagon.

I could guess where he was going. To Mrs. Holt's. Lately he spent every spare moment over there. I bet he took plenty good care of her oxen. I climbed out of the wagon. Addis had already dumped the crate on the ground and rushed off without so much as a glance at our poor teams.

The least I could do was comfort them. They stood patiently in their yokes as I stroked the soft white triangle on Rufus' nose. His red rimmed eyes looked at me reproachfully as if the bad road were my fault. It was the same disapproving look Pa had given me this morning when I handed him his coffee.

Yvette had already unpacked the kindling from under the wagon. As soon as she got the campfire going, she joined me.

Furious as I was at Addis, I still found myself making excuses for him. "Addis is coming right back to unhitch the teams. I guess we could water them in the meantime."

Yvette nodded without answering. We filled the two blue buckets from the water keg on the side of the wagon, and carried them back to the oxen. I didn't even use my crutches. Though it was a short walk, and I took it slowly, it was a very big triumph. And I had Yvette to thank for it. We stood side by side as Jackson and Ben slurped up the water from the buckets.

"What can I do about Pa, Yvette? Ever since I lied to him, he seems to hate me." It was all I could think about.

Yvette tipped her bucket so Ben could drink more easily. "I cannot tell you what to do, for I do not understand your father's anger. A Chinook father is never angry at his child and never punishes him. The child has to learn the difference between right and wrong for himself. If he makes a mistake and does wrong, the father explains what is the right way. But there is no punishment or blame. That is how the child learns the ways of the world."

It made sense. I had tried to talk to Pa, to apologize, but he'd only mumbled something and hurried away. That wasn't right either.

Yvette pointed to a rocky mountain peak that stood like a sentinel north of camp. Fremont's Peak, Pa had called it. Its summit was bare rimrock with dark green firs climbing its heights like moss on a boulder. At first I didn't see what Yvette was pointing to. Then I spotted a sudden rump patch of white high on the mountainside, then another, and another. It was a band of bighorn sheep, their brownish-gray coats the same color as the rimrock. They were leaping from ledge to ledge as if for the simple joy of it.

"Life is free for a Chinook child, like that," Yvette said as we carried our empty buckets back to the keg for refilling. "Then after his vision experience, the child becomes an adult, and what he does can be judged good or bad. But now he has a guardian spirit to guide him. With his new name, he is a new person."

I was about to ask Yvette when she would have her vision experience, but decided not to. I knew Yvette well enough by now to realize she told me only as much as she wanted to, and no more.

Rufus and Sock drank down the water we offered them, and bellowed for more. Yvette rubbed Sock's shoulder to quiet him, then stopped in mid-stroke. She lowered her head and half shut her eyes, closing down her face in that private expression I had come to know. I turned around to see what had put her on guard. Stephen Meek was riding up on his Indian pony, the silver ornaments on his bridle glittering.

"Evenin', Miss. Is your father about?"

"He's on duty with the cow column," I answered curtly.

"I rode back here to tell you stragglers that we're passin' through a bad stretch of road now, but that it improves right soon . . ." Mr. Meek leaned forward in his big Mexican saddle and squinted at Yvette as if he were shortsighted. "Ain't that Dumelle's Chinook brat? I thought I told you to get rid of her."

An immense fury welled up in me. When I thought of all the hardship we'd been through on this cutoff, the terrible road that split open our oxen's feet, the heat, the poor grass, the broken wagons, and all because of Stephen Meek, I could have happily choked him with his own lariat.

"What we Thatchers do or don't do, isn't your affair. You can't order us about as if you owned us."

"Ella Jane!"

It was Ma's horrified voice behind me.

"Ma, you're back," I blurted out.

"Sarah Chambers is sleeping and it seemed foolish to wake her." Ma loosened her bonnet strings and looked from me to Mr. Meek, then back to me again. "Now what is this rude behavior all about, young lady?"

Mr. Meek slid off his pony in a noisy jangle of spurs. He was as angry as I was. "I told your daughter here to get rid of the Injun. I won't tolerate her travelin' in my caravan."

Ma laughed her short bark of a laugh and as soon as I heard it, I knew everything would be all right. She handed me her medicine case as if she were preparing for battle. "As I recall, Mr. Meek, we paid you $5 to pilot us on this cutoff. I'm sure you'd agree that we haven't hit such bad road since leaving the United States last May." Ma swept her arm out to include the stark rimrock mountains that heaved straight out of the earth, the sparse grass and the shallow muddy creek. "Now that you've led us into this God-forsaken country, I only pray you can find your way out as easily."

Hurrah for Ma. That would squelch Mr. Meek, all right. But Mr. Meek wasn't so easily put down. He walked right over to us, coming so close I smelled the tobaccoy-leathery-sweaty odor of him. He studied Ma as if taking her measure.

"It 'pears to me that the Injun gal is the issue at hand, ma'am, not the road. Bein' a greenhorn, it's likely you don't know that Chinooks trade in slaves. They buy 'n sell humans the way we buy 'n sell mules, but with far greater profit."

Mr. Meek was smart to size Ma up that way. Ma hated slavery just about more than anything in the world.

But Ma wasn't about to be put down either. She drew herself up to her full five feet eight inch height. "What Yvette's people do now or have done in the past is of no concern to me. I promised Yvette's mother to see her to a Christian haven, and I'll honor that promise. Now if you'll excuse me, I got a supper to prepare."

Ma started toward the wagon with her shoulders squared and her back straight as a soldier's. I was so proud of her I was ready to cheer. She had stood up to Mr. Meek and bested him. A grin spread across my face as I watched Mr. Meek mount his pony and angrily ride off.

I turned to Yvette, sure that she would be as pleased as I was, but she wasn't smiling at all. A terrible fury twisted her face as she watched Ma's retreating figure. Then Ma was in the wagon, and Yvette's awful expression of rage was gone. The long rays of the late afternoon sun must have been playing shadowy tricks, for now her cheeks dimpled as she returned my smile.

CHAPTER TEN

THE FOLLOWING NIGHT WE CAMPED
in a beautiful valley, green with thick grass and sweet water.
Running streams poked out willow-bordered fingers from nearby
rocky ridges. Signs of an earlier camp lay everywhere, trampled
grass, dead campfires, dried dung and bits and pieces of broken
wagon gear. But the valley was empty. Mr. Meek and the other
wagons must have stopped here, then pushed on.

I was alarmed. Though our two hundred wagons had started
on the cutoff together back at the hot springs, we'd soon broken
up into smaller companies of about thirty wagons each. We always
did. It made traveling easier. Now our little company, it seemed,
was at least a day or so behind the rest of the wagons. This past

week the narrow ravines and rocky Malheur River bed had forced us to travel single file. We must have been falling behind the whole time. Still, the road had been so bad, would have expected the others to have rested here a day or two to let their teams and stock recover. Then all two hundred of us could start out together again. That awful Mr. Meek had probably urged everyone on.

Ma didn't like it either. She banged the pots and pans as she pulled them from their crate. "We ought to stop in this valley for a while. Everyone needs a rest, and there's sickness in some of the wagons. Little Sarah Chambers is worse."

Yvette was unpacking food for supper. "Does Mrs. Chambers have children?"

"Yes, a girl of three and a boy of one," Ma answered.

"Why, they're just the ages of Lucy's children," I exclaimed.

Ma nodded thoughtfully. "Yes, they are, aren't they?"

"Do you mean your sister Lucy?" Yvette asked, surprising me. She had never been curious about our family before.

"My dearest, oldest sister."

Ma paused, a frying pan in one hand and the coffee pot in the other. "Sarah reminds me of Lucy. I never realized it before, but they both have that same fair skin and frail look about them."

It was true. I remembered the day I'd seen Mrs. Chambers washing at the hot springs with Ma and mistaken her for Lucy.

Ma frowned. "Sarah's chills and fever are bad today. Maybe I'd better go to her right now. Ella Jane, you can be in charge of supper and the Bible reading tonight."

When Ma didn't give me any further instructions, I knew she was really upset. She just picked up her medicine case and hurried off.

As soon as supper was over, Pa lit his pipe. Ever since I'd lied to him, he'd practically ignored me. Now, when he stood up, he didn't even look my way. "I won't stay for the Bible lesson tonight. There's a card game I'm going to."

66

Addis stretched and got up, too. "Why don't you just forget the Bible lesson, Ella Jane? I'm gonna take a walk."

Which left Yvette and me. And Sparky. Sparky needed exercise and I needed Sparky. She was always such a comfort, and tonight I needed comforting badly. I fetched her from the wagon. Though she still hadn't learned to sit up and beg, she'd been cooped up in her cage all day. For tonight I'd just let her exercise. I scattered some pine cone seeds in her exercise basket and opened her cage door onto it. She scurried right out of her bedroom tin and into the basket. She balanced on her long tail as she stuffed the seeds into her cheek pouches. Her face swelled up as if she had mumps. I had to laugh at her thrifty ways, as I closed the basket door and latched it.

The air had gotten so cool Yvette and I wore shawls. Though the chill discouraged the usual evening mosquito attack, nothing discouraged the hawks. They cruised, as always, in wide circles over-head in search of their next meal, and I was glad Sparky was safe in her basket. Yvette sat with her hands clasped around her knees as we watched Sparky scamper up and down her cedar tree branch. Yvette's brown legs and narrow feet looked wiry strong. No wonder she was such a fast runner. I studied my own leg. It was better, but it was still thin and white. I wondered if it would ever be as strong as Yvette's.

Yvette abruptly stood up. "The pots are dirty."

I had forgotten all about cleaning up. The cold stew would be hardened onto everything like flour paste. Yvette dropped all the pans and dishes into the cooking gear crate and headed with them toward the stream.

The orange sun was beginning to set in the pink and purple western sky. It was getting colder. Sparky seemed tired, and her little body quivered. She needed to be back in her bedroom cage, snug in her nest.

As soon as I settled Sparky, I tidied up the wagon. It gave me something to do to keep me busy, and with our tiny living space, straightening up was an endless chore. I had just finished repacking the food when I heard voices outside. I poked my head out the wagon cover. Ma had returned, and so had Yvette. Ma looked tired. Her eyes were ringed with dark circles, and wisps of hair straggled from her knot.

"Did you have a proper supper, Ella Jane, and Bible reading, too?" she asked as I climbed out of the wagon to join them.

She seemed distracted enough for me to give half an answer. "Supper was fine, Ma."

She wasn't paying attention anyway. "Sarah Chambers is dying, I fear."

"She is cold, then hot?" Yvette asked.

"Yes, and my calomel and wild quinine aren't doing any good."

"The bark of a certain willow tree can cut the fever, and it grows nearby, down by the creek where I washed the pots and pans."

Ma jumped at the suggestion. "You must mean the peach willow tree. That's so. I recall my grandmother using the bark to cure the intermittent fever. There's certainly no harm in trying it. Fetch me a knife from the wagon, Ella Jane, and I'll cut some now, before night falls."

"I'll come help, Ma," I offered.

The sky was darkening, with a tiny star blinking on here and there as Ma and I set out. The tall grass whipped against our skirts. It was so much easier walking on my leg these past few days, I was using only one crutch. As Ma led the way through a grove of alders, we heard the gurgle of water bubbling over rocks.

"Don't you think the rest of the trip will be easy going like this, Ma?" I carefully worded the question so that the answer would come out what I wanted to hear.

"I don't know . . ." Ma didn't finish. She stopped so suddenly, I bumped into her. "Addis!" she cried.

Addis? What was Addis doing here? I peered around Ma. I didn't see anything, but there was a rustling and commotion in the brush. After a moment, two figures struggled to their feet. Right away I recognized Addis' broad shoulders and green shirt. It took me longer to realize the second figure was Mrs. Holt. Her bright yellow curls fell over her face, and her dress was all twisted and rumpled. She brushed back her hair and straightened her skirts. Addis' clothes were mussed, too, and his copper hair was wild.

"Addis, how could you?" Ma sounded stunned.

Addis ran his fingers through his hair and walked toward us with a swagger. "What're you doing here, Ma?" His voice was unnaturally loud.

"You . . . you and that strumpet!" Ma spluttered.

"Now wait a minute," Addis protested.

"That woman is a harlot, an adultress, and you're no better." Ma almost spit the words out.

Mrs. Holt jumped out from behind Addis and lunged toward Ma. "How dare you call me names, you old crow? You think you're so high and mighty . . ."

Addis grabbed Mrs. Holt's arm and pulled her back. "Hush, Sophie, let me settle this." Addis didn't sound sixteen. He sounded sure of himself, like a man.

I couldn't see Ma's face, but her back was rigid with fury. "If you take that woman's side against me, Addis, consider yourself no longer my—"

"Stop!" I screamed. I knew what Ma was going to say and I didn't want to hear it.

Ma whirled around. She looked so surprised to see me, she must have forgotten I was there. "Ella Jane, go back to camp this instant."

I'd go, all right. I couldn't wait to go. I turned on my heel and loped away as fast as my one crutch would take me. I stumbled and tripped all the way back to the wagon.

Sobs choked my throat, but the tears didn't fall. I was too terrified for tears. Everything had happened so fast, I wasn't even sure what it was all about. All I knew was that Ma and Addis had hurled terrible, hateful words at each other. I wished I'd never heard them. But I had, and they repeated themselves over and over in my head.

CHAPTER ELEVEN

ADDIS DIDN'T COME BACK ALL NIGHT, but he must have been watching our wagon the next morning. As soon as Pa went out to bring in the teams and Ma left to check on Mrs. Chambers, Addis appeared to pick up his belongings. I begged him to come back to us, to make up with Ma, but he wouldn't listen. He was determined to stay with Mrs. Holt, and the more I argued, the angrier he got.

It seemed like all the world was angry. Pa still wasn't talking to me for lying to him, and now he was furious at Ma that Addis had left our wagon. Pa needed Addis to help drive the teams, set up camp, keep the heavy water keg filled, make repairs on the wagon. Without Addis, Pa would have a hard time managing.

Now that we had started following the Malheur River again, I was beginning to understand why malheur meant ill luck. As soon as we broke camp in our beautiful valley, we picked up the river's north fork, and for the next two days traveled over the worst road we'd hit on the cutoff yet. The river led us through impossibly steep rock canyons. On one stretch, the chasms were so narrow, we had to take to a bluff that ran beside the river, then head down another ravine back to the river bed again.

To spare the oxen, I got out of the wagon and walked as much as I could. At least the effort of walking kept me too busy to brood about how far our company was falling behind the main caravan. Mr. Meek left notes for us describing the route ahead, so we knew we weren't forgotten, but they were two days ahead of us now. All I cared about was catching up, but we couldn't seem to do it. As soon as we started to make good time, something always happened. On one steep turn, Mr. King's axletree broke, and our whole company was delayed while the men fixed it. Then two of Mr. Dawson's oxen gave out, which meant we had to wait while the Dawsons moved all their belongings to the Hosford wagon and continued the journey with them.

At the end of two days of walking, I was so done in I could scarcely eat my supper. As soon as we finished cleaning up, I climbed into my tent and wrapped up in my blanket roll. But my body was one giant ache, and I couldn't fall asleep. I twisted and turned, trying to get comfortable. When that didn't work, I forced myself to lie perfectly still and watch the darkening sky. One by one the stars came out. By the time Yvette came to bed, the heavens were ablaze but I was still awake.

Yvette must have been tired, too. She worked on my leg without speaking or even singing. As she rubbed in the ointment, I noticed her breath puffed out in little clouds. Though it was only early September, the nights were terribly cold. Maybe it was cold enough to snow. I couldn't think of anything worse than being trapped in these mountains in a snowstorm. We'd never get out. Yvette could probably tell me when the first snows fell, but I was afraid to ask. I'd rather not know.

Half-expecting to see snow already flying, I peeked out of the tent. Instead of snow, I saw a tiny glow, like a new star, bob and weave around the edge of the wagon circle toward us. As it grew brighter, I realized it was a lantern approaching our tent. In its yellow dotted circle of light, I saw it was Ma holding her punched-tin lantern. As soon as I got a good look at her face, I sat right up. Yvette must have sensed something wrong, too. She sat up beside me.

"What is it, Ma?"

She didn't answer. Instead, she suddenly went limp and fell to her knees. The lantern slipped from her hand. I quickly reached out to steady her, then righted the lantern. Tears were running down her face. I stared in astonishment.

"Ahh, it is the halo wind," Yvette said softly, her voice almost like a breath of wind itself.

"What do you mean?" I demanded.

"Yaka wind halo chako. It means her breath does not come. She no longer breathes. She is dead." Yvette's voice was still a whisper.

"Yes, it's true," Ma sobbed. "She died. Sarah Chambers died."

Sarah Chambers! Why, Ma hardly knew her. They'd only met this past month. Ma hadn't even cried when her own father died.

Yvette moved closer to Ma. "It was like watching your Lucy die, wasn't it?"

"Yes, yes, Lucy," Ma cried. "My Lucy is gone."

What was wrong with Ma? Lucy was safe with her husband and babies on her farm in Illinois. "Lucy's fine, Ma. She's home with her family."

It was as if Ma hadn't heard me. "They were so alike, both brave, but frail. It might have been Lucy there, fighting for every breath. I tried my best to save her, but nothing helped, not even the willow bark."

I ached to put my arms around Ma and hug her, but she had

never held with that. Pa, I'd fetch Pa. I started to climb out of the tent, still wrapped in my blanket.

Ma grabbed my arm. "Where are you going?"

"To look for Pa. He's playing cards somewhere."

"No." Ma barked the word out. "It's his fault. Everything is his fault. My Lucy left behind . . . Benton . . . my own mother, almost blind . . . Mattie married. Now Addis is gone, too. It was wicked of your father to do this to us just because he's got the itch to always move on. Wicked. It will be the death of us all."

Ma didn't seem aware of either Yvette or me as the words tumbled out. In all my life, I had never heard Ma rave on so. I just stood staring at her, my mind shocked into a blank. If only I could wake up in my loft bed back in Illinois with all the family around me. But I couldn't. I was here, in the middle of nowhere, on the way to nowhere, with Ma half-crazy, and the rest of the family splintered and gone.

CHAPTER TWELVE

Ma INSISTED THAT MRS. CHAMBERS' grave have a headstone with her name and date carved on it. Before we'd started out last spring, we'd been told to leave no trace of a grave for the wild animals or Indians to dig up. But Ma was stubborn, and Mrs. Chambers had a proper Christian burial.

For the next three days, the road wound southwest through stony, steep terrain and low rimrock mountains. Though the approach to the mountains was gradual, they dropped off as steep as stair steps on the far side. We had to lock one, two, or sometimes all four wheels to ease our descent. Twice we had to unhitch our oxen and snub ropes around trees to let down the wagons slowly. With

Addis gone, Pa and Ma and Yvette and I had to do all the work, and it was backbreaking.

At last we were through the mountains. Ahead of us lay a wide, level valley. Timbered ridges stretched north and west of us. A big lake shimmered to the south, framed on the west by a huge mesa. The spongy, thick grass, crisscrossed with little streams, felt wonderful underfoot. Though Yvette and I had walked together all morning, we'd hardly spoken. Just putting one foot in front of the other took all our energy. But now, before we stopped for our nooning break, I had something to ask Yvette.

"Mrs. Chambers died four days ago, Yvette. When do you think Ma will be her old self again?"

Yvette was studying the landscape ahead as if she were looking for something. It wasn't until after she had scanned the whole valley that she answered me. "Your mother is troubled, not just by Sarah Chambers' death, but by thoughts of home and her family. It will take more time."

That wasn't what I wanted to hear. Though Ma worked as hard as ever, she didn't really care about anything. Every day she put on the same soiled apron, and fixed her hair so carelessly that by mid-morning it was all unknotted. She still read the Bible to us every night, but so listlessly, it was hard to pay attention. She even forgot to water her seedlings, and I had to take over their care. Pa was no help at all. When he wasn't working around the wagon, he was off somewhere.

"It's not like Ma to act this way. She's always been strong," I said, carefully looking around the valley myself in hopes that the main caravan would be circled there. Though I didn't spot any wagons, I did see a huge stick and mud beaver dam, and a beaver's head with its V-shaped wake breaking the surface of the pond. In the distance hundreds and hundreds of white water birds circled a large lake, their deep-throated cries echoing across the valley. A huge rack of what looked like elk antlers crashed off into the woods.

"Once my mother was strong, too," Yvette said, half-closing her

76

heavy eyelids in that way she had of drawing into herself. "Now my mother is weak. Instead of staying with her people, she left to follow her husband. Even when my father killed a Chinook and would not pay tribute to the tribe for the death, my mother did not leave him. Now her father Dusdaq will not take her back even if she wished it. Once my mother was beautiful. Her legs were bound with ankle cords and her hair blew free. She wore dentalium shell necklaces and pendants and arm bands and bracelets and ornaments in her ears. She is ashamed now of her Chinook beauty."

I thought of Yvette's mother with her flattened forehead and tattoos, and beautiful was the last word I would have used to describe her. Still, I was surprised Yvette was so bitter toward her. I'd better drop the subject.

But I didn't stop thinking about my own mother. Yvette was probably right that Ma was upset about leaving everyone behind. Well, I couldn't do anything about Lucy or Benton or Grandma Fleming or Mattie, but I could do something about Addis. I'd have a talk with him, that's what I'd do, and try to persuade him to leave Mrs. Holt and come back to our wagon.

We circled for the nooning hour near a running brook. The valley was so beautiful, it seemed incredible the other wagons hadn't stopped here to rest, but they hadn't. Our scouts found a note from Mr. Meek buried at the foot of a stake describing the location and distance to the next camp. The note was dated three days ago! We were even farther behind than I feared.

With that on my mind, I wasn't very hungry. Ma just stared at her dinner and didn't eat much either. Pa rushed through his meal and hurried off. Yvette ate quickly, then she left, too, headed for the woods to find kindling. As soon as I'd washed the pots and pans, I started off on my own errand.

At nooning hour we just circled our wagons loosely without fastening one wagon to the next with ox chains the way we did at night. I knew right where Mrs. Holt's wagon was. Addis always camped at the opposite side of the wagon circle from us. To avoid meeting up with Mrs. Holt, I walked the long way around. We had run into each other yesterday, and Mrs. Holt had stuck her nose up in the air as if I were some nasty, crawly creature. I put my nose up in the air, too, but she'd already turned her back and missed my snub.

Luckily, just as I approached her wagon, Addis climbed down, carrying his rifle. His ammunition pouch hung on his belt and his powder horn was slung over his shoulder. He saw me and frowned. "What're you doing here, Ella Jane?"

"I got to talk to you, Addis."

"I'm going hunting."

"Let me come with you. I can be quiet."

Addis didn't say yes and he didn't say no, so I just followed along. I hoped it wasn't far. I was tired after walking all morning, and Addis took long strides. We trudged along in silence. Now that I'd come, I felt suddenly shy. Though Addis had been gone less than a week, he seemed older and more manly. Or was that my imagination? Whichever, I'd best get on with the matter at hand.

"Ma and Pa want you to come back to our wagon."

Addis stopped short and glowered at me. "Did they say that?"

"Well, not exactly, but Ma's been real unhappy lately. She cried about your leaving."

Addis laughed as if he didn't believe me.

"She did. I heard her. I know she wants you to come back." The noon sun was right overhead now, blazing down on us.

"Is Ma willing to apologize to Sophie Holt?" Addis asked.

I didn't even have to answer. We both knew there was no chance of that. "Couldn't you come back to our wagon without a fuss, Addis? The road's been so bad, we need your help."

We had arrived at a grassy mountain meadow beyond the beaver pond. Addis took a good look around. Then he loaded his rifle and lay down on his stomach in a protected hollow, tall grass on all sides hiding him from view. He glared at me over his shoulder.

"I'm tired of hearing about this, Ella Jane. Now either hush up or go back to camp."

I dropped my crutch on the opposite side of the hollow from Addis and threw myself down beside it. I picked up a blade of grass and began to chew on it. Now what? Now nothing. All I'd done was make Addis madder than ever.

I propped my chin in my hands and stared across the green meadow. It buzzed with a million bumblebees darting in and out of the red clover. Then I realized the whole field was alive, not just with bees, but with tiny mice and rabbits and birds and butterflies. Grasshoppers and katydids and crickets zipped through the air, setting up a raspy serenade. A grove of aspen trees shimmered in the sunlight just beyond the meadow. A Steller's jay squawked and took off from one of the trees. Something must have startled it. I looked closer. There, to one side, I saw figures moving in the shadows of the aspens.

Careful to stay out of sight, I peered over the tall grass. Two Indians mounted on ponies were talking to someone on the ground. I didn't even have to see the blue calico dress and thick black braid to know it was Yvette. She had a certain way of standing forward on her toes that I recognized right away.

But who were the Indians? Maybe I should point them out to Addis. He still faced in the opposite direction and hadn't noticed them. Then I remembered that someone had said harmless digger Indians lived in this country. They were simple people, who wandered around practically naked, roasting crickets and digging camas bulbs for food. Yvette had probably come across them while she was out gathering kindling and asked for directions. Of course, that's all there was to it. Addis would just get excited if he saw the Indians, and with that rifle in his hands, there was no telling what he might do.

Anyway, Yvette seemed to be saying good-bye to the two men. They exchanged hand grips. Then the Indians walked their ponies out of the aspen grove and turned west so their faces were in profile. Their heads were shaped almost to a point, and they weren't half-naked at all. They were handsomely dressed in rabbit skin robes that reached to their knees. They weren't digger Indians, they were Chinooks, that's what they were. But Chinooks lived in the Columbia River basin, not around here.

I watched the two Indians until they had ridden out of sight. So did Yvette. As soon as they were gone, she began to gather twigs and sticks for kindling. I ducked low behind the tall grass so she wouldn't see me. Long after she had filled her basket and headed back to camp, I lay still, trying to make some kind of sense out of what I had just seen.

CHAPTER THIRTEEN

IDIDN'T KNOW WHAT TO DO. HALF
of me was itching to ask Yvette about the two Indians. The other
half of me didn't want her to know I'd been spying on her. I decided
not to mention it. After all, two Indians on horseback weren't all that
alarming. We'd seen plenty of Indians before, sometimes as many as
four or five, following our caravan for days. For sure, two lone
Chinooks weren't about to attack thirty armed wagons.

As it turned out, the next day I didn't get a chance to talk to
Yvette at all. She was sick. She insisted on walking in her usual
place, but she was barely able to keep up with the teams' slow pace.
Her dark skin was sallow, and her usually clear eyes looked as dull
as the oxen's. Even her glossy black hair seemed lifeless. She refused

breakfast. The nooning meal came and went, and so did supper. Still she didn't eat.

"I hope Yvette's not down with the mountain fever," Ma muttered as she and I washed up after supper. "There's sickness in the company, and after losing Sarah Chambers, I can't bear to have anything else happen. Yvette had best spend the night in the wagon."

I was lonely sleeping outside by myself. For the past two weeks now, Yvette had worked on my leg every night. Sometimes she sang to me and sometimes she told me a Chinook tale. I liked the stories best. "Now that night has come, my tale can begin," she always started. Without Yvette's company, I was sure I wouldn't get to sleep, but I must have been tired. I dozed right off.

I don't know what woke me. One minute I was asleep, and the next I was wide awake, my whole body alert. From the next tent I heard Pa's rattling snore. South of the wagon circle, one of the night guards was quietly playing a flute. I knew neither of those familiar sounds had awakened me.

Then I heard it. No wonder I'd roused with a start. A coyote was howling. It wasn't so much howling as that weird singing I'd heard twice before. Stankiya's spirit-power song, that's what it was. I pulled my blanket tight around me and waited for the next eerie notes.

Though I didn't wait long, this time it wasn't the coyote I heard. It was a rustling noise behind me, the sound of the wagon cover being opened. My tent faced the campfire, away from the wagon circle, so I couldn't see what was happening, but a moment later, Yvette tiptoed past carrying an iron pot and dipper. I dropped my head down on my arms so as to appear asleep, but I slit my eyes open to watch. As the coyote set up his singing cry again, Yvette bent over our campfire.

The red embers lit up her face. It was aglow with excitement, a half-smile showing her even white teeth. Instead of wearing her usual braid, her hair was loose, parted in the middle and tucked behind her ears. She scooped up a dipperful of hot coals, dropped them in her iron pot and closed the lid. Then, in that special springy way she had of running, she sprinted off in the direction of the desert.

Yvette was going to her vision quest. I was as sure of it as if she had told me. As a matter of fact, I had been told, by Stankiya. I didn't stop to think. I just threw a blanket over my shoulders, slipped my bare feet into my shoes and started after her.

She was running north. She had to be headed for that small fresh-water lake north of camp. There was nothing else but desert and sagebrush for miles around. Right after leaving the wide valley yesterday, we had hit this high desert country with its endless horizons broken only by distant rimrock mountains.

A jet-black skyfull of brilliant crystal stars and a white half-moon lit my way as I hurried along. I did my best not to think about all the little night creatures scurrying underfoot in every direction. At least it was too cold for snakes. And it was cold. As I stopped to wrap my blanket tighter around me, I heard the coyote again. He was definitely north, and closer. All of a sudden I stopped short and looked back. I had followed Yvette without thinking, but now the wagon circle was hidden from view behind me, and Yvette was nowhere in sight. Still, I'd come too far to turn back now. I had to keep going.

Guided by the North Star, I kept walking north. Gradually, the hard ground underfoot gave way to softer bottom land. Reeds and scattered cattails began to take the place of sagebrush. It was amazing how the desert grew almost to the edge of this little marsh lake. I was nearly there. Slowly, I crept closer. I stopped short. Not twenty feet away two huge swans slept on a big stick and grass nest, their heads tucked under their wings.

There was a sudden flutter and splashing just beyond the swans, near the edge of the lake. Ducks and geese, startled from their sleep, pushed off into the water with a great quacking and squawking. At the noisy commotion, the swans were startled awake.

"Ko-hoh, ko-hoh!" they trumpeted as they both took off, their great wings thrashing. Their big feet pushed at the water as they slowly lifted into the air.

By now, every bird on the lake was awake and in flight with a thunderclap of gabbling voices and beating wings. Something had disturbed them. The half-moon threw enough light for me to see two small fires burning, one to my right and one to my left, on either side of the lake. Though Yvette must have built them with the hot coals she'd taken from our campfire, I didn't see her anywhere. Then I noticed a form bigger than any bird moving through the water. Yvette was swimming in the lake.

That in itself was incredible. I had never known anyone in my whole life who could swim, and that water must be freezing cold. Even now, with a blanket around me, I was shivering. Yvette's head suddenly sank beneath the water. She was drowning. I couldn't swim, but I had to do something. I crashed through the tule rushes toward the lake just as Yvette's head broke the surface in a shower of silvery drops.

"Masasa!" she cried.

I dropped down behind the tall rushes and watched in silent amazement. Yvette dove under the water again. This time I wasn't so alarmed, but I still held my breath until she surfaced.

"Masasa!" she shouted again.

I watched, not thinking, not fearful, not anything but spellbound as Yvette slipped under the water again and again. Five times she dove and five times she sprang from the water crying, "Masasa!"

Then she was swimming for shore. She stumbled out awkwardly, as if the muddy bottom were sucking her back in. I was surprised to see she was naked, the water glistening off her body as if it were greased. She headed for the little fire on the right bank of the lake. She must have made it of sagebrush stems. Even from where I hid, a good two hundred feet away, I smelled the familiar stench of burning sage. Slowly Yvette circled the fire, around and around.

84

"Masasa!" she called out on each turn.

Still naked, she waded back into the lake and swam to the opposite bank. Again she staggered out of the water as she headed for the second fire. This time I counted as she circled. Five times she walked around the fire, crying "Masasa!" on each turn.

She stopped. She leaned forward, on guard, as if she were listening for something. I strained to listen, too. Most of the ducks and geese were still circling overhead. Some had returned to their nests, and a few were swimming quietly around the edges of the lake. Then I heard it, a deep-throated growl. There was a sudden movement behind Yvette, out in the desert. It was an animal, darting, weaving, backing. It was the coyote! As he padded closer and closer to Yvette, his eyes gleamed lantern-bright in the firelight.

I had to be crazy. That coyote might attack. Bobcats, wolves, panthers, all kinds of wild animals could be prowling nearby. Even the skirrings and squealings of the little familiar night creatures sounded loud as animals roaring. Still, I didn't move. I couldn't. My eyes were fixed on those two glowing eyes as if I could never pull away. Just then Yvette raised both hands above her head.

"It has begun!" she cried out. She fell to the ground, her arms outstretched before her.

The coyote didn't move and neither did Yvette. But I had to get out of there. Slowly, slowly, I backed out of my hiding place in the tule rushes. Bent over in a crouch, I was still retreating backwards long after the ground was rock hard underfoot and the little marsh lake was out of sight behind a hill. Only then did I turn around, and head south toward camp. Though I was stiff from squatting so long in the rushes and my leg hurt, I made even better time returning than I had on my way out.

Then I was back. I crawled into my tent, exhausted, my body damp with sweat though I was trembling from the cold. I lay still as a stone in my blanket roll for a long, long time. The moon had already set when Yvette, dressed again in my worn blue calico dress, returned to the wagon as secretively as she had left it.

CHAPTER FOURTEEN

WHEN THE REVEILLE GUN FIRED THE
next morning, I was so tired I could hardly get up. My mind had
been circling for hours . . . the coyote . . . Yvette's swim in the
lake . . . her walking around the fires. But her cry, "It has begun!"
concerned me most. I tried to figure it out. She might have meant
her Chinook adulthood had begun, or that Stankiya was now her
guardian spirit. Or maybe it had something to do with us on the
cutoff. We were still in high desert country. The marsh lake where
I had followed Yvette last night was the only fresh water for miles
around, and that didn't make sense. Though we should be nearing
the John Day River grasslands by now, the country was becoming

86

more barren and arid. If only our company could catch up to Mr. Meek's caravan, we'd at least know what was happening and where we were headed.

Ma was already up and dressed when I finally climbed out of my tent twenty minutes after reveille had sounded. She looked tired, and her usually straight back was stooped. She didn't even mention my being late. "Dress quiet, Ella Jane. Yvette's still asleep," she called as I headed for the wagon wrapped in my blanket.

Though it was already past five, the eastern sky was only beginning to lighten. The September days were getting shorter. I knew the sun would soon warm the air to hot, but right now, it was freezing cold. I rushed barefoot across the hard ground.

Yvette was asleep on the mattress, her hair spread loose over the pillow. She lay on her back so strangely rigid, it alarmed me. I bent down to make sure she was still breathing. Yes, her chest rose and fell gently.

I dressed quickly, anxious to get out of the wagon. I had already started to climb down when I remembered I hadn't fed Sparky. I reached up on the shelf, opened her cage door, and threw in some dried fruit and seeds. I'd give her water and fresh straw later, when Yvette was awake.

But Yvette slept on, through breakfast and through all the noise and confusion of packing. When Ma stepped down from the wagon after putting away the breakfast gear, she looked worried. "Yvette's still fast asleep. I pray to God she hasn't got the mountain fever like some of the others."

I stared at Ma. Yvette wasn't sick. How could I have forgotten? She had told me the day before and the day after a vision experience, the vision seeker fasted and slept. I opened my mouth to tell Ma, then bit it shut. Ma might understand visions in the Bible, but Yvette swimming around naked in a lake was something else again.

But Ma never missed anything. "What's wrong, Ella Jane?"

"Ah . . . nothing, Ma. I was just going to say I'll walk this morning so Yvette can use the mattress."

87

"You look bone-thin, Ella Jane. You're not sick, too, are you? If anything happened to you . . ."

"Oh, no, ma'am. I feel fine and my leg is better." It was true. Despite all the walking I'd done these past days, my leg really was stronger and today I planned to use no crutches at all.

Ma and I walked in Yvette's usual place beside the rear left wagon wheel while Pa drove the oxen. For months now, his shouted orders had been enough to keep the teams going. Now they'd grown so weak, he had to use his whip. I turned my head away every time I heard it whistle through the air and smack against their bony flanks.

Once the sun was up full, the desert shimmered under its strength. There was nothing to see in any direction but sagebrush and the distant black rimrock mountains. A hard west wind blew a fine alkali dust straight at us. My ears were caked with it. My eyes stung, and even my teeth tasted gritty. And the weight of the oxen and the heavy wagons crushed the gray, dry sage so that the smell of it stung my nose.

Because we were at the end of the caravan as usual, we had to battle everyone else's dust and dirt. At least those ahead broke through the mule-high sagebrush for us. Addis and Mrs. Holt were probably near the front. Addis didn't like to be last at anything. Addis. I wondered if he would ever come back to us. He was so mad, it would take a lot of doing. It would take an apology from Ma to Mrs. Holt, that's what it would take. Would Ma ever go that far? I doubted it, but I had nothing to lose by trying.

"Maybe Mrs. Holt isn't so bad, Ma. She's pretty enough."

Ma pulled her kerchief up higher over her face and didn't say anything.

"Addis grew up fast, Ma. He was bigger than Pa at fourteen. I remember you laughing about it."

Ma nodded and smiled. "I remember."

"Recall how Addis liked Sally Meade back home? I guess Addis has always been partial to girls."

Ma was still smiling. "Addis never was like Benton. Benton was so backward, he up and married the first girl who took a fancy to him."

A sudden gust of wind blew something in my eye that smarted so much I had to stop. Ma stopped, too. I tilted my head back for her to take a look. She held my eyelid up and flicked out a little insect with the corner of her kerchief. It left my eye teary and sore, but I couldn't drop the subject of Addis while Ma was being so agreeable.

"With Mrs. Holt traveling alone, Addis probably wants to protect her, Ma, like it's his Christian duty. All Addis wants is an apology from you to Mrs. Holt . . ."

"That's enough!" Ma grabbed my shoulders and spun me around. All I could see were her bloodshot eyes above her kerchief and the frown lines that creased her forehead. "This business with Addis has nought to do with you, Ella Jane. I regret you even know of it. Now I forbid you to mention it again. Ever."

I swallowed hard. "Yes'm."

We hiked the rest of the morning without talking much about anything. The heat, the smell of the sage and the endless track of desert sapped our strength. I was so parched, I couldn't even make spit to rid my mouth of the taste of dust. Once I was sure I saw a lake sparkling in the distance, reflecting a mountain and green trees. Then, as we approached, I realized it was only my eyes playing tricks. After that, I saw more phantom, faraway lakes that glittered cool, then disappeared as we drew close. Water was all I could think about, though there weren't any clouds in the sky that even held the promise of rain. I longed to wake Yvette and ask her how far it was to water, but Ma wouldn't let me.

We didn't stop for our nooning break until two that afternoon in the hopes we'd find telltale green grass that would show us where to dig for underground springs. Finally, the teams were so done in, we had to circle our wagons into a dry camp. I went about my noonday chores as usual. It was easier to keep going than to brood about what might lie ahead. I envied Yvette sleeping through it all.

I was just watering Jackson from the bucket when our two scouts came riding into camp on their sweat-soaked horses. All of us, men, women and children, rushed around them.

"There ain't a sign of water anywheres ahead, and no note from Meek as to where we should camp for the night. His trail leads due west into the desert."

No one looked at anyone else as we went back to our wagons. It was too frightening to discuss. Walking into the punishing west wind all morning had been bad enough, but the thirst made it almost unbearable. Now we couldn't even count on water ahead. Though our lips were swollen and cracked, none of us had to be told to drink sparingly from our water kegs. And oh, how my leg hurt. The whole length of it ached. Still, to spare the oxen, I knew I had to walk the afternoon distance.

But Ma wouldn't let me. "Ella Jane, I want you to ride in the wagon this afternoon, regardless," she ordered as we got ready to start.

I didn't argue. I didn't think I could walk another step. Yvette was still in that strange, deep sleep when I climbed in the wagon. Her lips were moving as if she were dreaming.

"Masasa," she mumbled.

Masasa was the word she had shouted over and over last night. "Yvette?" I called softly.

She moved her head from side to side without opening her eyes. "Non, Yvette. I am Masasa."

Masasa must be her new name. Yvette had said a vision seeker always took a new name. But I had awakened her. She blinked her eyes open.

"Are you all right, Yvette?" I whispered, though there was no one around to hear. I felt strange with her, as if she were a different person altogether.

"I am only weary." She sounded the same as ever. She looked the same, too, as she turned over and fell back asleep.

She must never, never know that I had followed her on her vision quest. The whole experience was already blurred in my memory, like one of those make-believe lakes that shimmered blue and fresh in the distance, then mysteriously faded away.

For the time being I'd better take care of Sparky. At least I didn't have to worry about her. She was used to this terrible heat and drought. Still, she needed fresh water and straw for her nest. I reached up for her cage. As I lowered it from the shelf, the little door swung back and forth. It was unlatched, and the metal clasp Addis had made for the cage door was missing. Hardly daring to breathe, I lifted the lid off her bedroom tin and checked all around her corner nest. The tin was empty. Then I took the top off her storeroom tin. It was full of nuts and seeds, but nothing else. Sparky was gone!

CHAPTER FIFTEEN

I MUST HAVE LEFT SPARKY'S CAGE open this morning when I fed her in such a hurry. If only she hasn't been out of her cage long, I prayed. She just had to be somewhere in the wagon.

"Tsst. Tsst. Tsst." I clicked my tongue against the roof of my mouth in our special signal. I didn't care if I woke Yvette or not. I had to find Sparky. I ran my hand along the shelves hoping to come across her soft little body huddled in a corner, but all I found was dust. Though Ma had Yvette and me clean the wagon every day, the fine alkali dirt coated everything. Even now the west wind snapped at the wagon cover so that the gray dust sifted right in. Armfuls of dust wouldn't have bothered me if only I could find

Sparky, but she wasn't on any of the shelves. I'd have to search the whole wagon.

I spent what was left of the afternoon poking in every nook and crack where she might be hiding. Despite the racket I made, Yvette slept on. I searched through the crate of cooking gear, in the laundry tub, behind our clothes, in the blanket rolls, under the washboard, in the coffee grinder, around Ma's seedlings, in the butter churn, inside boots, any place she could burrow. I even opened the false floor where Pa kept his whiskey jug, Ma hid her silver and candlesticks and extra food supplies were stored.

I didn't find Sparky, but I was surprised to see how little food we had left. The bacon was almost gone, and the flour sack was nearly empty. In fact, everything was low but the beans and the pemmican. I was so tired of beans, I would have been happy to run out of them. As for the pemmican, I didn't know what it was before starting this trip and I wished I'd never found out. We'd learned to make it from the Indians. Dried meat was pounded into powder, mixed with a hot fat and dried currants, then pressed into loaves. It made a hopelessly dry and tasteless dish.

When I closed the trap door, I realized I had covered every inch of the wagon and Sparky was nowhere to be found. All of a sudden, I felt queasy. The hot air was thick with the smell of worn boots and the dirty clothing we hadn't been able to wash since the hot springs. Mosquitoes and insects had gotten into the wagon so that my arms and hands and even my legs were swollen with bites. My clothes clung to me, and my hair was wet against my face. I had to get fresh air.

I opened the wagon cover and climbed up on the wagon seat. The sun was blinding. It had sunk so low in the western sky, we were riding straight into it. At least the wind had died down so that we weren't pelted by the usual dirt and sand.

Pa still trudged beside the oxen, though he was filthier than ever, and the team's pace was even slower. The other wagons, all ahead of us, seemed more spread out now, each trailing its own cloud of dust. White swirls of alkali powder blew off distant flat, dry lake beds. Stretching endlessly ahead, I saw the trampled sagebrush and wheel ruts that marked the route Mr. Meek and the earlier wagons had taken. At least we were still on their trail.

The sunset was the usual wild burst of pinks and oranges and purples I used to think was beautiful. Now I'd give anything to see the gray skies of Illinois as heavy thunderclouds rolled in and lightning crackled. I remembered the wet coolness of raindrops on my face and the squish of mud through my bare toes. I could almost smell the clean freshness of soaked earth after a heavy rain.

The image was so clear in my mind, I looked up, half-expecting to see rain clouds overhead. Instead, I saw three turkey buzzards outlined against the metallic sky. With their huge wings motionless and their pink claws tucked under their bodies, they circled patiently, as if waiting for some poor animal to die so they could eat it. At the sight of them, everything came back with a rush—the desert, my thirst, my shaky stomach and aching head. And Sparky. All of a sudden, my stomach heaved. I leaned over the side of the wagon and threw up.

Pa must have heard me. He halted the teams. "Hester, see to this child. She's sick," he called back to Ma.

In seconds Ma was beside me on the wagon seat. My nose was running and my eyes watered. I longed for a drink to rid myself of the terrible taste in my mouth, but I had no voice to ask for it.

"What is it, Ella Jane? Are you sick like Yvette?" Ma asked.

It took me a moment to answer. "No, Ma, it's just that the wagon was so hot and airless, it made me dizzy." I smiled the best I could to show her I was all right.

I couldn't bring myself to tell Ma that Sparky was gone. Once I said it out loud, then I knew it would be true. If I didn't say it, I could still believe Sparky was safe, and I would find her.

Pa must have known how I craved a drink. He brought me a gourdful of water from the keg. It was soupy and warm, but I drank it all down.

94

Ma handed the gourd back to Pa. "John, we got to stop for a while. It must be well past six. The teams, all of us, need rest and food and I want to brew some calomel tea for Ella Jane and Yvette . . . and me."

I was surprised by the "me." I turned and looked at Ma, really looked at her. As soon as I saw her eyes, I knew it was Ma who was sick, not Yvette or me. Her eyes were more than bloodshot from the wind, they were yellowish, and ringed with heavy, dark circles. For the first time, I realized her hand on my arm was hot and dry. And trembling.

Pa had already cracked his whip and gotten the teams started. "No, Hester," he answered. "We lost time fixing the wagon tongue at nooning hour and the rest of the company is all ahead of us. We got to push on."

It was true. We were falling behind. I'd walk. I'd do anything to help us go faster. I started to climb off the wagon seat when Ma moaned and swayed against my shoulder. Then her full weight was on me, and I was falling under it.

"Pa!" I shouted.

Between the two of us, we carried Ma into the wagon. Though she looked as if she'd lost weight lately, she was tall and big-boned and heavy to lift.

"Yvette," I called. "Wake up. We need the mattress for Ma."

Yvette had slept all day. She wasn't sick. I knew it. She could get up and walk with me.

It was as if Yvette were already awake. She sat right up. Her eyes were clear, and her cheeks bright with color. She got to her feet quickly without any of the grogginess I always felt after a long sleep. As Pa and I eased Ma onto the mattress, Yvette stepped aside and began to braid her long hair. In spite of my concern for Ma, I noticed how well Yvette looked. Her eyes almost sparkled. They were as deep, deep brown and lustrous as her sea otter robe, and I wondered how I had ever thought they were yellow.

I undid Ma's dress and took off her bonnet while Pa awkwardly stood by. As I unbuttoned her shoes and slipped them off, Ma started shivering.

"I'm cold," she whispered.

"Cover her," Yvette said, handing me two quilts from the trunk.

Ma raised her head and looked up at Pa as I tucked the quilts around her. "I'm so weary, John. Can't we stop here a bit while I gather my strength?"

Pa rubbed his side whiskers the way he did when he was ill at ease. He was always uncomfortable around sickness. "I'm sorry, Hester, but we got to push on." He cleared his throat as if he were going to say more, then changed his mind and backed out of the wagon. I followed and grabbed his arm to stop him.

"Pa, we can't go on. Ma's not just tired, she's sick. Her skin's hot to the touch, and she's got the chills."

Pa wouldn't meet my eyes. He held onto the wagon seat, then swung to the ground. "I'd stop if I could, Ella Jane, but we got to push on."

"We got to push on." It was like a refrain. If Pa said it one more time, I would stamp my feet and holler. Then my anger was gone, and a sudden panic swept over me.

"Mr. Meek has gotten us lost, hasn't he?"

Pa wouldn't even acknowledge my question. He just picked up his whip and headed toward the teams.

"Yaaa-ho!" he shouted louder than he needed to as he whacked his whip on the animals' scrawny backs. That told me more than anything. Pa and I were alike that way. If Pa didn't say we were lost, then for him, it wouldn't be true. But I had seen the look in his eyes, and I knew we were lost just as sure as if he had yelled it at the top of his voice. I braced myself on the wagon seat so as not to fall. Of all the terrifying thoughts that raced through my head, only one stood out clearly—Yvette's cry last night at the lake, "It has begun!"

CHAPTER SIXTEEN

It WAS THE FIRST TIME SINCE WE started out last May that we traveled any distance at night. Yvette and I walked while Ma rested in the wagon, not quite asleep, but not really awake, either. I kept checking on her, though I didn't know what to do beyond cooling off her hands and face with a damp cloth.

Each wagon hung a lantern from its rear axle as a beacon for the wagons that followed. Because we were the last wagon in line, our lantern lit the way for the cow column trailing behind us. Twice that night we stopped to water the teams. Yvette and I drank, too, swishing each tepid mouthful around and around in our mouths before swallowing. Pa hated to stop for even that long, and so did I. I was terrified those lantern lights ahead of us would fade from sight.

I felt strange walking along with Yvette. Though she looked the same, I knew she was different. A vision experience changed a person forever, that's what she'd said. I didn't want to be the first to speak, but there was something I had to ask her. I cleared my throat self-consciously.

"Yvette . . . you say you know this country . . ."

Yvette nodded without answering.

"Mr. Meek is going in the right direction, isn't he?" I asked, not sure that I really wanted a reply.

I needn't have worried. Yvette didn't answer directly. "The desert is large. Much of it looks the same as every other. Meek, I think, is confused."

"Maybe there'll be water soon." I tried to sound casual.

"Water is always scarce in the desert."

It was as if we were both tiptoeing around a sleeping baby so he wouldn't wake and start screaming. Since we had no choice but follow Mr. Meek's trail anyhow, I let it drop at that. It was hard enough just to keep going. The moon and stars mocked us with a brightness that shed no warmth at all. Though the wind died down after sunset, the desert cooled off so fast at night, Yvette and I were bundled up in shawls and Pa's wool shirts. Still, we were cold. And terribly tired. If only we could ride Pa's horse, but Mr. Field had borrowed Campbell this past week to help drive the cow column after his own horse broke his leg and had to be shot.

Ma was on my mind, too. I had always taken her good health for granted. Now she was sick, really sick. I couldn't help remembering poor Mrs. Chambers. A child had died as well, the Packwood baby, according to a note we'd found from the main caravan. But Ma wouldn't die. She just couldn't. Yvette had said malheur meant ill luck, and we'd had enough of that already without something happening to Ma.

"You seem sad. Were your thoughts of Sparky?" Yvette asked in a gentle voice. "You will find another to take her place."

"No." Sparky was special. She could never be replaced. Even now I could almost feel her sharp little nails run up my leg as she dove into my apron pocket for seeds.

"I understand. Sparky was your prized belonging."

Sparky had been my darling pet. I had never thought of her as my prized belonging, but I guess I could have called her that. Yvette had a strange way of expressing herself. I recalled she said that to own another's prized belonging was to gain that person's power. Still, I had never owned Sparky, I had only cared for her. Considering the way I'd left her door open, I hadn't even done a very good job at that. But I never left her cage door unlocked. Never. Not even when I was in a hurry like early this morning. I glanced at Yvette, puzzled. Yvette had been asleep the whole time I was searching for Sparky, and I hadn't told anyone that she was missing, not even Ma. There was no way for Yvette to know . . .

I was being silly. Ever since we'd started this cutoff, I'd been suspicious as an old spinster. Yvette had noticed Sparky's empty cage with its unlocked door, that's all.

"Cr-r-ruck!"

I cried out in alarm as a huge black bird, bigger than a crow, flew into the air with a flurry of beating wings not ten feet ahead of me.

"It is only a raven," Yvette laughed as the bird flapped away into the night.

But I was trembling, and my scream had frightened the oxen. They tossed their heads and bellowed in alarm.

"You girls get on that wagon seat and ride," Pa yelled back. "I got problems enough without you spooking these animals."

Pa made it sound like riding was a punishment. That was all right with me. Yvette and I scrambled up on the wagon seat. It was such a relief to sit, I just closed my eyes and let my body sway with the motion of the wagon. Yvette put her hand lightly on my arm.

"Let me tell you a night tale as we rest." Though Yvette's voice was too low for Pa to hear, it had that same faraway lilt it always did when she told one of her stories.

"Raven was a very vain bird as well as clever," Yvette began. "Before the Great Transformer sent Raven to earth, he told his helpers to make Raven the most colorful bird of all. They worked hard, and after many moons, Raven was so beautiful, even the bluebird and cardinal looked dull beside him. But Raven was not happy. First he wanted his wing colors changed. Then he wanted his tail feathers brighter. The helpers made all the changes. Still, Raven was not satisfied. Finally the helpers went and told the Great Transformer of their difficulties.

"When the Great Transformer went to their workroom, he found Raven looking like a beautiful rainbow. But the bird told the Great Transformer he wanted still more changes before he would go down among men.

" 'Such a vain bird needs only one more change,' said the Great Transformer. He gave his helpers a brief command. They threw soot and ashes all over Raven until he was black as night. Black he was when he was sent down among men, and black he is today."

I smiled at the ending. Yvette knew just how to cheer me up. The huge bird that had terrified me only minutes ago, now seemed only foolish.

"It is always folly to want more than one has been granted," Yvette said. "The greedy Raven had everything to make him happy. When he demanded more, he ended up with less."

"I guess so," I agreed. Yvette's stories were like Ma's Bible lessons that always had to have a double meaning. Only Yvette's stories were new to me, and more fun.

We rode on now in silence, too tired to talk. I checked the position of the Great Dipper around the North Star and guessed it was past midnight. I watched the other wagon lanterns flicker in the distance until they hypnotized me into a kind of numbness. Half of me kept my balance on the narrow wagon seat, while the other half of me dozed.

"Whoa, there."

Vaguely I was aware of Pa halting the teams. Then as the wagon creaked to a stop, I heard the thrum-thrum of hoof beats. By the light of the moon, I saw a rider approaching. My groggy mind somehow decided it was Addis returning to us. Then I blinked and took another look. It wasn't Addis. It was a man I didn't know reining up his horse to speak to Pa.

"Are there any more wagons behind you?" the man growled.

"Are you from Meek's caravan?" Pa asked.

"Aye, we're camped 'bout three miles up ahead. We been there near four days now. You got more wagons behind you?"

"No, we're the last, except for the cow column to the rear. Did Meek find water?"

The man grunted. "Aye."

Water and the safety of the main caravan lay ahead. At the promise of fresh water, the juices started up in my parched mouth.

"There's two good springs, but now, includin' your company, we'll have close to two hundred wagons and over two thousand in stock usin' em." The man shook his head. "The sharin' will be hard."

"But Stephen Meek . . ."

"Meek!" The man spit the word out. "Meek got no idea where we are, and we can't move 'til we're sure there's water ahead. So far, we ain't found a drop in any direction. Meek left yesterday to search farther out. If'n he comes back without finding water, by God, we'll lynch him."

Pa, Yvette and I just stared at the rider as he angrily turned his horse and rode back into the night.

CHAPTER SEVENTEEN

I WAS SO ANXIOUS TO REACH THE
Meek camp, those last three miles seemed endless. Finally we were
there. Rings of glowing campfires showed us how all the different
companies had coiled into separate circles, so we pulled into our
own circle, too. After these past lonely days of travel, the sight of
all those white-topped wagons reassured me. Lost or not, this many
people were bound to find water somewhere.

Yvette and I slept well past dawn. I woke first, turned over and
was about to go back to sleep when I remembered Ma. I had to
check on her. I tried to be quiet as I crawled out of the tent, stiff
and sore as if I'd been bucked off a horse, then rolled on.

On my way to the wagon I noticed Pa's tent was empty, and he

102

was nowhere in sight. Afraid that something had happened to Ma, I yanked open the wagon cover. It was all right. Pa wasn't inside, and Ma was sleeping. But her breathing was labored, and her damp hair stuck to her face. She must have heard me. She opened her eyes and ran her tongue around her cracked lips.

" 'Morning, Ella Jane," she whispered. "Did we find Mr. Meek's camp or was I dreaming?"

"No, Ma, we caught up to the main caravan and we're all here together." There was no need to mention we were all lost together, too. "We're camped by two good springs, so I can fetch you a drink of fresh water."

Ma tried to smile. I knew how thirsty she must be. I was that thirsty myself. I wondered how I had spent all my thirteen years before this without giving any thought to water. For weeks now, the lack of water, the promise of water and where to find water had never been off my mind.

I filled the pitcher from the water keg on the side of the wagon. Why, the keg was almost empty. Pa hadn't refilled it yet. The rider last night had said there were two good springs, but until I saw our keg full of clean, fresh water, I wouldn't believe it. Pa never should have gone off without taking care of it.

I stomped back into the wagon with the pitcher, trying not to let Ma see how annoyed I was. She drank so eagerly, the water spilled down the front of her dress.

"I'll change you into your nightdress, Ma, and now that we got plenty of water, I can bathe you, too."

When Ma didn't put up an argument, I knew she was really sick. Sobered, I emptied the water into the wash basin and dipped a clean cloth into it. Having the mattress on the floor made it hard for me to work, and since kneeling was awkward, I half-sat, half-stooped as I bathed Ma's arms and legs. The heat of her body dried the water right up. She must be terribly feverish. Ma ought to have medicine and proper care. I remembered Pa saying Doctor Wilcox had taken the cutoff. I'd go find him as soon as I was finished.

Knowing Ma would want to look presentable, I quickly dressed her in her nightdress, then leaned over to pull out the dirty sheets to change the bed. As I yanked on the sheet, something that had been wedged between the mattress and the wagon frame, flipped out. I picked it up. Right away I recognized the metal clasp to Sparky's cage. The mystery was solved. I must have been playing with Sparky on the mattress and dropped the pin. But that wasn't possible. Sparky had only been missing since yesterday, and I hadn't been on the mattress for two days.

Even sick, Ma didn't miss much. "What is it, Ella Jane?" she asked hoarsely.

"Nothing, Ma. I was just thinking about breakfast." I slipped the pin in my apron pocket and finished changing the sheets. There, Ma was all set.

Now it was time to find Dr. Wilcox. Though I was rattled by my discovery, I'd just have to put it out of my mind until Ma was taken care of. I climbed down from the wagon and stood a moment to get my bearings. We were camped on the eastern slope of a huge treeless, rimrock mountain. The springs must flow at its northern tip where a patch of grass and scrubby willows were a bright spot of green in the gray landscape.

The main camp was between our company's wagons and the springs. As I headed toward it, I realized I hadn't seen this many people since the hot springs. But at the hot springs, everyone had been excited about starting on the last leg of their trip. No one looked excited now. The women dragged around with untidy hair, cleaning up after breakfast. The children weren't playing hopscotch or blindman's buff or leap-frog or anything. They just sat. Even the men were standing idly around. With their half-grown beards and dirty clothes, they looked like last year's scarecrows. A skinny dog sniffed at a pile of slops. A couple of makeshift privies had been thrown together beyond the wagon circles. A line of men stretched in front of one, and a line of women in front of the other.

There was Mrs. Holt's wagon camped with the main caravan.

104

Addis must have done that just to avoid us. I didn't see Addis or Mrs. Holt, but I did see my friend Mary Herren, seated on the tongue of her wagon trying to soothe her screaming baby sister. She didn't notice me, and for now I didn't have time to stop and talk. Still, I couldn't help noticing how bad Mary looked. Her yellow curls hung limp under her soiled bonnet and her cheeks were chapped raw by the sun and wind. Her arms and face were stick-thin.

I wondered if I looked as awful as Mary. Probably. If everyone else had changed, I must have, too. As far as I could tell, the only thing that never changed was the wind, the everlasting wind. Even now it tossed smoke and ashes and trash and dust and the stench of burning sagebrush stems into a smothering haze.

If we ever reached the Willamette Valley, I never wanted to smell a sagebrush fire again. *If* we ever reached the Willamette Valley. Last night I had been comforted by our numbers, but now when I saw how discouraged everyone was, I felt discouraged myself.

I approached an old woman who was tending a pot of lumpy mush. "I'm looking for Doctor Wilcox. Do you know his whereabouts?"

The woman jerked her head west toward the mountain. "One of the men got hurt in a fall, and the doc went to see to him."

That meant I had to cross the main camp again. I'd rather walk around the outside of the wagons. As I passed the last wagon in line and started out into the desert, I glanced up. Turkey buzzards wheeled overhead. Everlasting wind and everlasting turkey buzzards. Somehow turkey buzzards always reminded me of Sparky. Poor Sparky. I wondered where she was now. Strange how I'd found that cage door clasp behind the mattress almost as if it had been hidden there . . .

Fifty feet or so ahead of me, something caught my eye, a figure running through the sagebrush. The blue dress was familiar and so was the graceful way the figure ran. It was Yvette. I had left her asleep, and now she was out here in the desert. I fingered Sparky's cage pin in my apron pocket. Yvette had every chance in the world to open Sparky's cage, then hide the pin.

I saw Yvette stop. Quickly I ducked behind a dusty clump of sagebrush and watched. Yvette looked west toward the mountain, then raised both her arms above her head in a gesture of greeting. She was holding a rifle. Right away I recognized the long, slender curly maple stock and bright-polished brass patch box and trim. It was Pa's rifle! That rifle meant more to Pa than anything in the world. Shading my eyes against the glare of the sun, I tried to see what Yvette was waving at. Something moved about halfway up the mountainside, but I couldn't make out what it was through the waves of heat that shimmered off the desert floor.

My vision blurred with the strain of trying to see. I rubbed my eyes, then looked again. Now Yvette was gone, and Pa's rifle was gone with her. Pa's treasured rifle. The sage grew so tall here, she could be anywhere. It didn't matter. If I had to, I'd look behind every shrub to find her and get Pa's rifle back. As I started to poke around the nearest sagebrush, I heard a strange noise. It was a dry, whirring sound, familiar and yet not familiar.

"Do . . . not . . . move." It was Yvette's voice. Over to my right, she slipped out from behind a clump of gray sage. Pa's rifle was raised to her shoulder and she was aiming it toward me.

"Do . . . not . . . move," she said again, just as deliberately as before.

There was a rushing in my ears as if terror were a wave crashing in my head. I couldn't have moved if I wanted to. Yvette was going to shoot me!

P O O O W W W !

The sound exploded with the fury of a cannon. Noise, smoke and the smell of gunpowder stunned me. I fell back, tripped on a root behind me and crashed to the ground. I landed so hard I didn't even notice I'd twisted my bad leg under me. Yvette put down Pa's still-smoking rifle and walked toward me. She stopped about a yard away, and with her bare foot, kicked something out from behind a rock. It was a three-foot-long snake with its head blown off. Yvette reached down, picked up its tail and shook it. Its gray sectioned rattle clicked dryly. A rattlesnake! It had been coiled in my path ready to strike, and would have struck if it hadn't been for Yvette.

CHAPTER EIGHTEEN

U NTIL I STOOD UP I DIDN'T KNOW how badly I had wrenched my leg. It was as if a pair of pincers was squeezing it. Tears sprang to my eyes as I grabbed Yvette's arm.

"Please," I begged, "help me back to the wagon."

Without answering, Yvette put her arm around my waist and I leaned against her. We hadn't gone more than twenty feet when I held up my hand for us to stop.

"I forgot. I have to find Doctor Wilcox for Ma."

Yvette brushed a strand of hair back from my forehead. "Don't worry. I will take care of you both."

She sounded so sure of herself, I believed her, mostly because

I wanted to believe her. Right now all I cared about was getting back to our wagon. We made it in better time than I had hoped, but as soon as I saw Ma lying there on her mattress, tears filled my eyes again. I wanted to throw myself down beside her and cry, but I couldn't do that. She was too sick, and besides, Ma didn't take to crying.

"I was almost bit by a rattlesnake, Ma, but Yvette killed it and she saved my life and I hurt my leg again," I blurted out all at once.

Ma's eyes were hardly open, but I knew by the sudden spots of color on her cheeks that she had heard me. "Can you put any weight on your leg?" she whispered.

I nodded. "Some. But you should have seen that snake, Ma. It was horrible. It was the same gray-green color of the sagebrush so that I would have stepped right on it. Yvette said it was all wound up ready to strike. If she hadn't shot its head off, it would have bit me." Just talking about the snake made me sick to my stomach, and I could hear that dry buzzing even now.

Ma looked me over from head to foot as if to make sure I was really all right. Then she turned to Yvette. "How can I thank you? God blessed me with seven children. Two died, and the rest are scattered. Ella Jane is all I have left, and she is dearer than life to me."

Ma's voice was so weak, I thought I hadn't heard her right. Was she talking about me, Ella Jane, who wasn't gentle and kind like Lucy, or beautiful like Mattie, and who always had to be nagged into doing the chores?

Yvette kneeled down by the mattress and picked up Ma's square, work-scarred hands in her two small brown ones. "I would like something from you in return."

Ma didn't hesitate. She just nodded.

Yvette leaned over Ma so their faces were only inches apart. "I am Chinook, a proud people. Belongings mean wealth to a Chinook, and I own nothing. If I owned your Liberty Chest, I would arrive at the mission school with pride, not as a beggar. Give it to me."

Ma's Liberty Chest. It had been in the Fleming family seventy years, and Ma had cherished it her whole life. Ma would never give it to Yvette. Never.

Ma closed her eyes. It was so still in the wagon, I heard the wheeze in her chest as she breathed. All the camp noises sounded far away, as if the three of us were trapped in a canvas-topped cocoon, sealed off from the rest of the world. At last Ma opened her eyes. "The Liberty Chest is yours, child. Take it with my thanks."

Yvette bit her lip in her two front teeth and quickly glanced down at the floor. Though her dark lashes fluttered like black wings against her flushed cheeks, I had seen an expression of triumph light up her eyes.

Ma must be delirious with fever to give away her Liberty Chest. No, her face was serene. She seemed no more upset than if she'd discarded an old dress. I meant that much to her. I hated to think of Ma losing her Liberty Chest, but now at least I knew how much she loved me.

"I shall now prepare your medicine," Yvette said. She was already going through her basket of belongings. Then she rummaged around in the top drawer of the Liberty Chest where all Ma's herbs and medicines were kept. It was strange to see Yvette pull open the forbidden drawer. Well, it was her drawer now. She mixed everything together in a bowl, adding water from the pitcher drop by careful drop. When she was finished, she held out a spoonful of thick yellowish liquid to Ma. Even from where I stood, I could smell its strong, unpleasant odor.

Ma raised her head and looked at the spoon. I knew she was deciding whether or not to take it. I was about to say how the ointment for my leg smelled bad, too, when Ma opened her mouth like a baby and Yvette slid in the spoon.

Then it was my turn. As Yvette sat me down on the leather

trunk, I was surprised to realize I was shivering. The wagon had heated up with the mid-morning sun, but I was cold deep down in the very marrow of my bones. Yvette must have sensed it. She covered me with a quilt, then tucked another quilt behind me to support my back.

She gave me such a wide smile, her cheeks dimpled. My teeth weren't even, so I always noticed how straight Yvette's were, except for the little chip off her front tooth. And they were white as bleached bones on the desert. What a ghoulish comparison. Whatever made me think of it?

Ma was already asleep as Yvette began to soothe my leg with her ointment. She must have known how much it hurt because she didn't work long. When she was finished, she held out a steaming mug of some kind of brew. I had the dreamy sensation that everything was out of my hands now as I drank it down obediently. It was bitter, but I finished it all.

"Rest . . . rest . . . rest . . ." Yvette crooned as she pulled the quilt back over me.

And rest I did. I slept on and off all day, with no idea of time or place. I was only drowsily aware of what was going on outside, the shouts and talking, angry voices, laughter, the howl of the wind plucking at the wagon cover. From time to time, Yvette roused me to drink more of the bitter brew. I dimly knew that she was tending to Ma as well.

Sudden loud voices startled me awake. They were right outside the wagon, and one of them was Pa's. I sat up, feeling refreshed and surprisingly wide awake. Even my leg felt better. I hadn't thought of Pa all day, and now he was back. It was almost dark outside as he stepped into the wagon. The small lamp Yvette had lit made his shadowy form seem enormous as he greeted Ma.

"Did the doc come? You look better, Hester." He kept running his hands through his hair in a distracted sort of way.

"I feel better. Yvette has taken care of me." Ma sounded better, too.

Pa began to pace up and down, but the space was so small, he could only take a few steps before he had to turn and start in the other direction. The floor boards groaned under his weight.

"I rode out today with some of the men to find water." Pa spoke quickly as if he were in a hurry. "We rode due west without finding a drop. Meek and his group searched north with no luck either. They came into camp right after us. A mob of men was waiting for Meek, and when they heard he hadn't found water, they lit out after him. They're claiming Meek's never been in this country before, that he talked everyone into taking the cutoff just to get the money for the pilot's job. If they find him, they may very well kill him."

I didn't want anyone killed, but after all, it was Meek who had gotten our two hundred wagons into this fix. I couldn't blame the mob. I felt almost that violent toward Meek myself.

Ma propped herself up on her elbows. Her gray eyes looked huge in her pale face. "Where are the Meeks now?"

"Mrs. Meek is safe with the Hancocks. Stephen Meek is hiding in Packwood's wagon, but everyone knows they're friends. They'll hunt him down there, for sure."

Ma and Pa exchanged a look. They didn't agree on much, but I was certain they agreed on this. I was right. "Fetch Meek. He can stay here with us," Ma ordered.

Pa nodded and moved to the back of the wagon where his rifle usually hung. "Where's my rifle?"

Pa's rifle! I hadn't thought about it since Yvette killed that rattlesnake this morning.

Yvette walked right up to Pa and boldly faced him. "I left your gun outside. I shall go find it." Without waiting for his answer, she picked up a lantern and slipped out of the wagon.

Pa's big frame seemed to grow larger as if he were swelling with rage. "What is she talking about, my rifle is outside?"

Ma reached up from where she lay and pulled at his trousers leg. "Hush, John, the child saved Ella Jane's life. She killed a rattle-snake with your rifle, and in the excitement must have forgotten it.

She'll find it, and even if she doesn't, you can replace it. And there'd be no replacing Ella Jane."

Pa had been so cross at me lately, I wasn't sure he'd want to. That was silly. Of course he would. Gradually Ma and I calmed him down, explaining what had happened, and how Yvette had broken Ma's fever with her medicine, and cared for me all day as well.

While one part of me was praising Yvette, another part of me was thinking about Pa's rifle and how the gunsmith had fashioned it to Pa's bidding. That rifle was Pa's most prized belonging, just like the Liberty Chest had been Ma's, and Sparky had been mine. Now Yvette owned the Liberty Chest, and Sparky was gone. I remembered how I'd found the clasp to Sparky's cage door behind the mattress where Yvette had lain for two days, and I knew in my heart that no matter how carefully Yvette or any of us searched, Pa's rifle would never turn up.

CHAPTER NINETEEN

IT DIDN'T TAKE PA LONG TO GET Stephen Meek. Mr. Meek was as brash as ever. He marched right over to Ma and tipped his big hat.

"Evenin', ma'am. I appreciate this. We seem to have a little misunderstandin' here that needs some straightenin' out."

Misunderstanding! This whole cutoff was a misunderstanding, and it was all Stephen Meek's fault. I hoped he didn't tip his hat and speak to me or I just might tell him what I thought.

"Hasn't Yvette come back with my rifle yet?" Pa demanded, though he could see plain enough that she hadn't.

Mr. Meek scowled. "Is Dumelle's brat still with you?"

I didn't see that Mr. Meek was in a position to complain about anything, but apparently he felt differently. His leathery face reddened. "So she's the reason why those two Chinooks have been followin' us. They ain't let us outta their sight since the hot springs. I even seen them watchin' us here. I couldn't figure it out, seein' as how this ain't Chinook country. I thought I told you to get rid of . . ."

"Enough!" Ma struggled to sit up. She was so angry, she forgot to cover up her nightdress. "That child saved my daughter's life, and her medicine broke my fever. I'll hear no more about her."

I wasn't listening to Ma. I was thinking about those two Chinooks. If Mr. Meek said they'd been following us since the hot springs, it was a good bet Yvette had been meeting them all this time, too.

Ma wasn't finished. "You owe us an explanation yourself, Mr. Meek. Where are we now, and how far is it to water?"

Mr. Meek was as scrappy as a fighting cock. "I said there's water ahead and there is. I just got to get my bearings to find it."

At that moment, the wagon cover snapped open, startling all of us. What a relief to see it was only Yvette climbing back in the wagon. As soon as she closed the cover and turned around, she found herself face to face with Mr. Meek. Sparks practically flew between them. Yvette's whole body tensed right up, and the scar over her eye pulled into a tight line.

Pa grasped her arm with his big hand. "Did you find my rifle?"

"Non, it was too dark. I will search on the morrow," Yvette answered in the stiff manner she always used with Ma and Pa. Slowly she backed up, then turned to leave the wagon.

"Where are you going?" Pa demanded.

"I left the lantern in my tent. But it is dark in here. I will fetch it." Yvette quickly climbed out of the wagon, and pulled the cover shut behind her.

"You may spend the night here, Mr. Meek. In the morning, when tempers have cooled, you can give us all a full accounting." Ma's voice was firm, but she sounded tired, and her face looked gray as she sank back on her pillow.

"Look, I didn't even have to come back to camp. My wife and me could have ridden north outta here any time," Mr. Meek retorted. "You don't have to worry. I'll get you to The Dalles like I promised."

At that moment, Yvette returned with her lantern. Now there were five of us crowded in the narrow space. Pa started to assign sleeping arrangements. "Ella Jane, you and Yvette sleep in your tent as usual. Meek, you'll have to stay here in the wagon . . ."

"Hush," Ma interrupted. "Listen."

Outside we heard a humming buzz. It was hard to tell where it was coming from, but it wasn't far away.

"Quick, douse the lights," Meek ordered. He grabbed the lamp and snuffed it out. Yvette hurried to the back of the wagon, then blew out her lantern. We were in instant darkness. The menacing sound grew louder, like an angry swarm of attacking hornets. Only as it drew closer, the hum became a muttering of angry voices. It must be the mob.

"We want Meek," someone yelled right outside our wagon.

"We know he's in there, Thatcher, send him out."

Lights from lanterns and pine knot torches circled our wagon until we were surrounded. The men's shadows played on the wagon cover like dancing night demons.

"Meek! Meek! Meek!" a voice shouted. The others picked up the cry until they were all chanting. "Meek! Meek! Meek!"

The whole wagon vibrated with the refrain. Out on the Great Plains I'd once seen a pack of wolves finish off an old buffalo. The wolves had worked together, cutting off the buffalo's escape route. Then they had snapped at him from every direction until he fell. I had that same trapped feeling now.

"There must be near a hundret of 'em out there." Mr. Meek didn't sound brash now.

"We won't give you up to any mob." Ma's voice wasn't very loud, but she sounded as if she meant it.

Pa groaned. "If only I had my rifle."

I was glad he didn't. If one person fired, everyone might start firing. Please, I prayed, no shooting.

At that moment, the wagon gave a terrible lurch as if we had ridden over a big stone. We tipped to one side, then landed back on our wheels with a bone-jarring thud. I was pitched to the floor. Pa was thrown off balance, too. He must have tried to catch himself. I heard a wagon bow snap under him as he crashed back against Ma's seedlings.

There was laughter from outside. "Awright, Meek, if you won't come out, we'll rock you out," someone yelled, and there was more laughter.

Somehow their laughter was more terrifying than their anger. I had to get out of here. Hardly noticing the pain in my leg, I started to crawl across the floor. I bumped into something solid. It was Ma. She must have been rolled off her mattress onto the floor. She was tangled up in her quilt and struggling to free herself.

I was trying to help Ma when the wagon started to rock in the other direction. This time we tipped so far, we almost went over. Everything in the wagon crashed to the floor, the looking glass, tin cannisters, pots, pans, the chamber pot, tools, lamps, the washboard, the hourglass, the butter churn. Pa slid toward Ma and me, twisting himself awkwardly to keep from landing on us. I held on tight to Ma as we were tossed back onto the mattress and slammed up against the side of the wagon. Sparky's empty cage flew through the air, whacking me hard on the shoulder. I heard a string of oaths from the rear of the wagon that must have come from Mr. Meek. Yvette was back there, too, but I couldn't worry about Yvette as we began to seesaw in the opposite direction.

"Hold onto the side of the wagon," I yelled at Ma, supporting her the best I could until I knew she had a good grip. Then I grabbed hold of the wagon frame myself.

Now everything in the wagon was falling the other way. I heard all the drawers crash out of the Liberty Chest. The trunk slid across the floor, battering into the crate of cooking gear. Why wasn't

Addis here to help us? Then I remembered Mrs. Holt's wagon was over in the main camp. Addis didn't even know what was happening to us.

"Stop! Stop!" Pa shouted. He was on his hands and knees trying to untie the wagon cover. As we started to rock again, the cover ripped open under his hands. Then I couldn't think of anything but bracing myself on the side of the wagon as Ma and I were hurled against it.

"Stop, for God's sake! The missus is sick," I heard Pa yell, but when I turned to look for him, he was gone. He must have jumped out of the wagon. Those men just might be crazy enough to kill him. They were still howling with laughter as if they were shaking ripe apples from a tree.

"Meek! Meek! Meek!"

Now we were pitching the other way. Broken glass tinkled. Pots and pans clattered as the trunk slid back across the floor. Then I was aware of someone crawling over my legs, past Ma and me toward the front of the wagon. From the light shining through the ripped cover, I saw it was Yvette. She reached the opening and clutched the torn canvas with both hands.

"Yeeoowwhhoo!"

Her cry was a wild animal wail, like a coyote baying at the moon. A chill shivered up my back. It must have had the same effect on the mob. Our wagon crashed back on its wheels.

Yvette scrambled out onto the wagon seat. She raised her hands above her head for silence. Stunned, Ma and I lay where we were, clutching the wagon frame as if our lives still depended on it.

"What's that Injun up to?" Meek growled from the back of the wagon.

Gradually, the noise and shouts outside quieted until the night was silent enough to hear the men sheepishly shuffle their feet and cough. Then Yvette spoke.

"I know the way to water and I can lead you." She didn't raise her voice, but I was sure that her words carried to the farthermost man.

There was a hush as if the men were trying to take in what she said. I was thunderstruck myself. If she had known where there was water, she should have led us to it long ago!

"Listen to her," Pa called out. "She's to be trusted. She saved my daughter's life today." I noticed that Pa didn't mention she'd lost his rifle today as well.

Again there was silence. Then someone shouted, "If you're so sure she knows what's she's talking about, then you go with her, Thatcher."

"Yeah, let Thatcher go."

"That's a promise," Pa yelled in reply. "I'll go with the girl tomorrow to find water if you promise to let Meek go free now."

"Why not?" a man laughed. "Meek ain't worth the rope it'd take to lynch him."

There was another humming buzz as the men started talking among themselves. Only this time the voices murmured reasonably instead of in anger. An "aye" or an "awright" sounded here and there in the crowd. Then I overheard a man right outside our wagon speak in a low voice to his neighbor.

"The Indian just might find water for us. After all, she was the one who told us where to find Meek."

I didn't know whether Ma heard or not. She still seemed so dazed, I was sure she hadn't. But I certainly had, and I felt as shocked as if the men had started to rock the wagon again. I knew Yvette hated Stephen Meek. I didn't like him either, but we all might have been killed. We almost had been killed.

I covered my face with my hands and began to cry. I cried and cried. I couldn't stop. Ma couldn't comfort me. Even when Pa came back in and said Mr. Meek had left and the men had taken their torches and gone away, I couldn't stop crying. Pa rubbed my head and called me his little Ellie Jay over and over. It was what I'd been waiting so long to hear, but still I couldn't stop. I cried for everything that was lost, for Lucy and Benton and Grandma Fleming left behind, and Addis and Mattie and Sparky and Ma's Liberty Chest and Pa's rifle and for us being lost. But most of all I cried for what I didn't understand, that we had taken Yvette into our family, and she had betrayed us.

CHAPTER TWENTY

Because Pa wanted to get an early start with Yvette, the three of us were up before dawn the next morning. We tried to be quiet so as not to wake Ma. Surprisingly, three men showed up to offer their help. Mr. McNary lent Pa his pack mule and rifle. Mr. Tetherow let Yvette ride his little mare, and Mr. Field promised to keep our water keg filled while Pa was gone. They didn't mention what had happened last night, but they acted as guilty as boys caught stealing in a melon patch. Their offer of help must have been their way of apologizing.

The closer Pa and Yvette were to leaving, the more I worried. Finally I pulled Pa to one side. "Please don't go," I whispered. "What if you get lost? You don't know anything about the desert."

"You heard my promise last night to the men, Ella Jane. I'd never go back on a promise." Pa's voice was so stern, I knew he was trying to make a point with me about keeping my word. There was no use arguing with him.

Besides, maybe Pa and Yvette would find water. Yvette seemed to know what she was talking about. She drew a map of their route in the hard packed dirt. They were to head north, then northwest past a ridge of volcanic mountains, and there, on a mountainside, about twenty-five miles from here, they'd find a creek hidden from the valley floor.

They just had to find water. This morning the pan of dishwater had a skin of ice on top and the horses puffed smoky clouds of vapor. If we didn't get out of here before the snows came, we might never reach The Dalles at all.

Dawn was just breaking in a gray sky as Pa and Yvette started off. Ma surprised us all by coming out of the wagon to wave good-bye. She looked worn and thin, but her color was better than yesterday, and her eyes seemed brighter.

"Look for my rifle, Ella Jane, and don't forget," Pa called back as he and Yvette rode off.

When their little caravan was out of sight, Ma and I sat on the wagon seat drinking our coffee and warming ourselves in the first feeble rays of the sun. I had packed the last of the coffee in Pa's knapsack, so we savored each swallow, knowing there'd be no more.

Camp was coming to life. Folks sluggishly stirred up last night's fires, drew water from their kegs, sent their children out to the herd to milk their cows. Everyone looked dirty and cold and tired. Lost Hollow was what they called this dismal place, and it was a good name.

No one even glanced our way. Maybe that was their way of pretending nothing had happened last night. I studied the different wagons, and wondered which men had been part of that terrifying mob. Old Mr. Walter, crippled by rheumatism, who hadn't played his fiddle in weeks? Mr. Henderson, whose daughter Addis fancied until he met Mrs. Holt? Mr. Stewart, with his two sick children? The more I thought about it, the madder I got.

"Ma, I can hardly believe what our neighbors did to us last night . . ."

Ma cut me right off. "Don't talk of last night. If we start laying blame, there's no end to it. Everybody went crazy with fear and worry, that's all. It's best forgotten and forgiven." Ma put down her empty mug. "Now let's get at tidying up the wagon."

Ma may have felt better, but what little color was left in her face drained to chalk white as she started to work.

"You'll just get sick again, Ma." I took the broom out of her hand and practically pushed her down on the mattress. She looked relieved when I covered her with the quilt, and gave her the yellow medicine Yvette had left for her.

"Hand me my Bible and spectacles, Ella Jane. It's not fitting the way I've neglected to read to you of late."

I never thought I'd enjoy Ma's Scripture lessons, but the sound of her voice and the familiar passages soothed me. And it took my mind off what I was doing. Ma was probably right when she said to forget what happened, but it was hard to be forgiving. An earthquake couldn't have done more damage. Part of the wagon was smashed where the trunk had battered against it. All the lamps, the hourglass and Ma's looking glass were broken. The chairs, table and bed frame weren't good for anything but kindling, and the middle bow of the wagon was split where it had given under Pa's weight. Even the binding on Ma's Bible was ripped and some of the pages torn loose.

After I swept up all the shards of glass and repacked what wasn't broken, I started to put the Liberty Chest together. Though I'd been curious all my life about what was in it, now I had the opportunity to find out, I wasn't sure I wanted to know.

I remembered that the herbs and medicines belonged in the top drawer. There were enough linens and lace and embroidered napkins and fine handwork yellowed with age to fill another drawer. Odd pieces of silver, strange foreign medals, two china figurines, steel needles and brass pins, a few gold coins, a pair of beautiful earrings and a matching brooch, all wrapped in lamb's wool, fitted into little compartments in the third drawer.

What was left was scattered across the floor. I carefully picked up old letters tied with ribbons, some in Pa's stiff handwriting and some in faded handwriting I didn't recognize. There were threadbare baby dresses, bonnets, rattles, Benton's and Addis' old exercise books, Lucy's, Mattie's and my first samplers, full of mistakes and rip-outs, gifts all of us had made years ago from nuts and pine cones and milkweed pods. Locks of baby hair had been lovingly folded in squares of linen, each labeled in Ma's neat stitching, Benton, Lucy, Matilda, Addis, Ella Jane. And Jesse and Rhoda Ann, too, the twins who had died as infants.

Stern, practical Ma had saved all these treasures. I didn't realize I was crying until a wet blotch fell on a teething ring in my lap. Quickly I looked up to see if Ma had noticed. Luckily, she'd fallen asleep, her spectacles halfway down her nose and the Bible moving up and down on her chest. I arranged everything back in the drawer and gently closed it.

It took me well past noon to finish cleaning up. There were some things I couldn't do, like repairs on the wagon bed and wheels. Even the heavy canvas cover took a man's strength to mend. I'd done all I could, and now it was time to look for Pa's rifle. I knew I'd never find it, but it was the last thing he'd asked me to do.

I took along one of my crutches. Though my leg was tired from bending and stretching, it was strong enough to do without crutches, but going out into the desert, I aimed to be prepared. Where there was one rattlesnake, there could be more, and I wanted a weapon. I headed for the outside of the wagon circle, walking with my eyes on the ground as I tried to remember just where Yvette had been standing when she had shot that snake. First she had waved Pa's rifle in the air, then turned . . .

I stopped short. Yvette had waved Pa's rifle in the direction of the mountain as if it were some kind of signal. And Stephen Meek had said he'd seen those two Chinooks right here, near Lost Hollow. Chinooks weren't supposed to be dangerous, but anyone was dangerous if they wanted to be. Why, Yvette could be leading Pa into a trap right now, just the way she'd led the mob to our wagon last night.

I had to do something, but what? I mustn't panic. I had to think straight. I had to get word to Pa, that's what I had to do. But how? Not through Mr. Meek. I didn't trust him any farther than the length of his ten inch spurs. For sure, I didn't want to worry Ma about it. Addis. An image of Addis' wide grin jumped right out at me. Addis was a man now. He'd know what to do. I headed at a run toward the main camp where I knew Mrs. Holt's wagon was circled.

I was so winded by the time I got there, I had to pause to catch my breath. Though the wagon cover was closed, I heard voices inside. First a man said something, then Mrs. Holt answered with a giggle. It must be Addis and Mrs. Holt. I was suddenly embarrassed, but I couldn't back down now.

"Addis?" I called hesitantly.

The murmur of voices continued. They didn't hear me. I stepped closer to the wagon and called louder. "Addis?"

There was silence, followed by a long minute's wait. Then Mrs. Holt stuck her head out the opening. She impatiently tucked a lock of brassy hair behind her ear when she saw me. "Whaddya want?"

"I have to talk to Addis. It's important." I had never wanted to sound more grown up, and my voice had never sounded squeakier.

"Addis ain't here."

"I thought I heard . . ."

Behind Mrs. Holt, the wagon cover was suddenly yanked open all the way. A dark bearded man glowered out at me. His dirty woolen underwear was unbuttoned at the neck showing a burst of curly black hair.

"You heard Mrs. Holt. He's on guard duty and ain't here."

The man snapped the cover shut, leaving me standing there with my mouth open. Then I heard the man laugh. "If'n that young cub had any sense at all, he'd be guardin' you, Sophie, not a herd of dumb animals."

I was furious. Sometimes it seemed like a black cloud of calamity had been following us Thatchers ever since we first saw that cursed Malheur River. Nothing had gone right for any of us. It wasn't that I didn't want Addis back with us. I just couldn't bear to see him hurt by someone as trashy as that awful Mrs. Holt. I felt like throwing a rock right through her closed wagon cover. Instead, I turned away. I couldn't waste my time on anger now, not when I still had to find Addis and tell him of my fears for Pa.

CHAPTER TWENTY-ONE

I FINALLY FOUND ADDIS ON GUARD
duty over a mile northeast of camp. I was glad I'd brought my
crutch after all. It was a long, hot walk in the afternoon sun.
Addis slid off his horse, Major, as soon as he saw me.

"What is it, Ella Jane? Is Ma worse?"

I was encouraged that Addis at least cared enough about us to
know Ma was sick.

"No, Ma's better . . . I came about Pa . . ." Now that I was
face to face with Addis, I didn't know where to begin. Best to go
back to when Sparky disappeared, I decided, and from there I went
on to how the two Chinooks had been following us, then to Ma's
Liberty Chest, Pa's rifle, Stephen Meek hiding in our wagon, and

I ended up by telling Addis how Yvette might be leading Pa into a trap right now.

Addis shook his head. "I can't believe that little gal's been up to all that mischief." He rubbed his sidewhiskers the way Pa did when he was thinking. "Still, I recall that night when you and Ma found Sophie and me down by the creek. I could'a sworn I saw Yvette spying on us just before you and Ma came along. Maybe Yvette planned it that way."

I remembered that evening as clear as if it had been last night. Yvette had come back from washing the pots and pans down by the creek, and told Ma about a willow tree growing there that would help Mrs. Chambers' fever. Ma and I had started right out for the creek and stumbled on Addis and Mrs. Holt instead.

"Yvette must have wanted us to find you," I agreed, "and she's probably setting a trap like that for Pa right now."

Addis put his hands on my shoulders, looked down at me and grinned his handsome grin that turned up one corner of his mouth more than the other. "This trip has been rough on you, hasn't it, Ella Jane?"

Addis and I had never kissed or even hugged, but on an impulse, I threw my arms around him. I felt his hard muscles under his shirt and his strength comforted me.

"Oh, Addis, I'm so afraid. I couldn't bear it if anything happened to Pa."

Addis returned my hug for just a second, then pulled away. "I'll start out after them as soon as I find someone to take my place here. I got my blanket roll with me and enough food to last two days, and I can fill my beef hides with water on the way. Pa and Yvette can't be traveling very fast if they're trailing a mule."

Good. If Addis left from here, he wouldn't have to go back to Mrs. Holt's wagon. Maybe by the time he returned, that horrible bearded man would be gone for good.

Addis packed quickly. When he was ready, I drew a map in the dirt just like Yvette's to show him the route. Then he was off. From a distance, he looked like a man sitting his horse, and the width of his broad shoulders was reassuring.

It was almost dark by the time I got back to our wagon, and the droves of evening insects had already appeared. Ma was swatting away at them as she stood over a simmering pot of beans. As soon as she saw me, she shook her big dipper. Where have you been? Why were you gone so long? Why didn't you wake me before you left? Ma may have still looked peaked, but she certainly sounded like her old self.

In a way, I wasn't sorry Ma had been sick. For the first time, I'd glimpsed the soft underside of her hard outer shell. Her fault-finding and harsh ways would never really bother me again now that I knew how much she loved me. I remembered the locks of baby hair, and knew she loved Addis, too. Right then, I decided not to tell her what Addis and I were up to. She'd only worry.

I rose early the next morning. I didn't expect to see Pa and Addis and Yvette much before noon, but at the slightest sign of activity in camp, I looked up, sure that Pa's little caravan had returned. Morning turned to noon, and noon to afternoon, and still there was no sign of them. I did everything I could to pass the time. I had a long visit with Mary Herren over in the main camp, but she was busy with her ailing baby sister, and somehow the two of us didn't have much to talk about. I even spent time searching the desert again for Pa's rifle.

The hours dragged. No one else in camp seemed to be doing much of anything either. Work used up strength, and strength took food and water. Our springs were still holding out, but we were all careful. Livestock needs came first, then ours.

I remembered how eager all these people had been to take the cutoff at the hot springs, and how they had mocked everyone else for following the old route. They'd made bets, too, on how much sooner our wagons would reach The Dalles than theirs. I sighed. Look at them now. Some, like old Mrs. Fanning, had given up. She spent every day propped in a chair, her eyes open, but not really seeing. Others, like Mr. Melvin, were always spotting imaginary sprigs of green through a spyglass, and trying to organize parties to go out into the desert to dig for water.

As for me, I didn't think I'd ever see green again. The whole world was gray, the desert, the sagebrush, the mountain, the dust, the animals, the wagons, me. So much dirt was caked under my fingernails, I was sure I'd never get them clean again.

Toward late afternoon, an approaching flurry of dust from the north sent my hopes soaring. Someone or something was coming. I raced all the way across the campground, only to find it was the Ownbey caravan straggling in. Mr. Ownbey had led thirty wagons with all their livestock out into the desert two days ago, determined to keep going until they found water. Now all thirty wagons were back. What animals hadn't died on the desert almost stampeded in their frenzy to reach the springs. One man was so exhausted, he staggered into camp, babbling like a drunkard. Most of the survivors weren't up to talking at all. They were a sobering sight.

As dusk fell, Ma couldn't hide her concern either. Her glance traveled north as often as mine did. And I carried double the burden. At least Ma was spared knowing Addis was out there, too. After supper, we sat by the campfire, hoping the smoke would drive away the insects. Ma read the Bible aloud, while I, desperate to keep my mind busy, worked on my hated sampler. But Ma didn't feel up to reading long, and she left to get ready for bed. I had just decided to forget the embroidery and get ready for bed myself, when Mary Herren appeared, carrying her baby sister Bethie. Mary's lips were cracked, and a red, sore-looking rash covered her arms and hands.

"Bethie's still sick, Ella Jane," Mary said. "She ain't eaten all day, and Mama figured your mother might have medicine to help her."

Mary began to cry without making a sound. Her tears left white tracks on her dirty face as they splashed into the baby's light fuzz of hair. "Oh, Ella Jane, what are we gonna do? We got almost no supplies left. Daniel's going out tonight to hunt porcupine for meat. Sarah Adams told me they had to eat their ox that died and it made her sick."

I put my hands on Mary's shoulders and looked her in the eyes just like Addis had done to me. "You got to have faith, Mary. We'll find water and make it out of here safe, I swear it."

I couldn't swear to it at all, but I didn't want to admit to Mary how scared I was, too. "Ma's in the wagon, Mary. Why don't you take Bethie in to see her?"

After Mary had disappeared into our wagon with the baby, I stared at the fading sunset, hating its beauty that promised nothing but another cloudless day tomorrow. I didn't even notice the Peterson boy run past until he called back, "Hey, Ella Jane, your father's jest comin' in."

Pa! I raced to the wagon. "Come quick. Pa's back," I yelled.

Ma burst out of the wagon, pulling a shawl over her nightdress. Mary, still holding the baby, was right behind her. Ma ran fast as a young girl across the campground with me right behind her. It was Pa riding into camp, but he wore a kerchief over his face and his hat was pulled so low, I wouldn't have recognized him if he hadn't been riding Campbell. Yvette was following on the little mare, leading the mule. Pa was leading a horse, too. It was Major, Addis' horse, and the saddle was empty.

I froze, one foot raised in front of the other, with my mouth half open ready to call a greeting. Then, as Pa rode closer, I saw he was riding double. Addis was slumped against Pa's back, his head wrapped in a bloody shirt and his eyes closed.

"Addis!" Ma screamed as she raced toward him.

Pa reined up Campbell. All I could see of Pa's face were his eyes, closed into painful slits. Ma reached up for Addis. Mr. Peterson and Mr. McNary hurried over to help. As they gently slid Addis off, he groaned and opened his eyes. He was alive. I went so weak with relief, I grabbed hold of Mrs. McNary for support. The men started back toward camp carrying Addis, with Ma walking alongside to cradle his head. Still, I couldn't move. It was as if my feet had taken root.

Pa didn't move either. He just sat slouched in his saddle as he pulled off his kerchief. His weather-chapped face sagged so that he looked like an old man. Yvette dismounted and walked toward me.

"What happened, Yvette?" My voice was a croak.

"The horse appeared at our camp last night. The saddle was empty. At daybreak we headed back to look for your brother. We searched all day. When we found him, he was hurt. He had been thrown from his horse."

Yvette frowned as if she knew I had sent Addis out after them. The thin scar over her eye tightened. "We had almost reached water when we had to turn back."

I wanted to believe they'd almost found water, but it was hard to believe Yvette about anything. Still, she had every right to reproach me about Addis. If I hadn't sent Addis after them, he'd be safe on guard duty now instead of lying unconscious, desperately hurt.

CHAPTER TWENTY-TWO

Someone fetched Doctor Wilcox, who decided Addis had a concussion of the brain. We were to keep water and vinegar compresses on his head and wake him from time to time in the night to make sure he wasn't still unconscious. I felt so terrible about what had happened, I insisted on taking care of him. Even Ma agreed I'd probably be able to stay awake better than she could.

I covered Addis with two quilts and wrapped up in one myself. I was glad it was cold. There wasn't anything else to keep me awake, but the cold. Though I heard the lowing and movement of cattle, no guards were whistling or playing mouth organs, and the usual camp night sounds were missing, too. All I heard was a child crying from nearby and his mother trying to hush him. It was as if the cold had driven everyone into hibernation.

Hardly a night passed without at least one or two coyotes talking it up, but toward dawn, I heard a special coyote. This one's familiar singing howls sent sharp prickles running up my spine. It was Yvette's coyote, Stankiya, and no doubt about it. He was back.

He kept up his wailing melody for long minutes, then stopped abruptly, the way he always did. Maybe Yvette was on her way out into the desert now to meet him. Though it would be easy enough for me to check her tent to see if she was gone, I decided not to. Taking care of Addis was about all I could manage for one night.

But the coyote's spirit-power song must have awakened Addis. He stirred and groaned. "Where's Sophie?" he whispered. "I have to see her."

I could have groaned myself. Of all the things he might have wanted, he had to go and ask for Sophie Holt.

"It's not yet dawn, Addis. I'll fetch her later."

That seemed to satisfy him. I changed the compress on his head and by the time I finished, he was asleep again. This time his breathing sounded deeper and more even. By now my legs were cramped from sitting so long, and my back ached. I creaked to my feet like old Mr. Walter and climbed out of the wagon to stretch my bones. The first gray stirrings of dawn were lightening the eastern sky. Another long day stretched ahead. I sat on the wagon seat and watched the sunrise. I didn't even notice Ma until I saw her hurrying toward me, a worried expression on her face. "How's Addis?"

"He's better, Ma. He's asleep now."

She nodded. "Good. I'll just look in on him, then go over to check on the Herren baby. You get some rest now, Ella Jane, and let Yvette cook breakfast."

After Ma was gone, I sat a while longer on the wagon seat until the sun was fully up. Ma wanted Yvette to start breakfast, but I wasn't even sure whether she was asleep or out chasing around in the desert. This time my curiosity got the better of me. I tiptoed

134

over to her tent, almost wishing she'd gone. Safe somewhere, but gone. The idea was so strong in my mind, I was startled to find Yvette fast asleep in her fur robe. I looked at her shiny black hair with its neat middle part and shook my head in bewilderment. Everything about Yvette puzzled me. She'd won Ma over completely these past few days, the same few days that she had baffled me by one strange action after another. Well, I had too much on my mind to figure things out now. With Yvette and Pa still asleep, and Ma gone, I'd better go fetch Mrs. Holt for Addis, like I promised.

I found Mrs. Holt all decked out in a red silk dressing robe standing by her campfire giving orders to a young girl cooking breakfast. And what a breakfast it was. My mouth watered just smelling it, bacon, flapjacks, blackberries and milk, stewed apricots, coffee. Mrs. Holt's head was bent over the fire, so she didn't see me. That was funny. With her head down like that, I could see her brassy gold hair had brown and gray roots. Mrs. Holt dyed her hair. I had heard of women doing that, but never, ever met one. At that moment, she straightened up.

"Well?" she barked when she saw me.

"It's Addis, Mrs. Holt." There was my stupid little-girl voice again. "He was thrown from his horse and got hurt pretty bad. He's in our wagon and asking to see you."

Mrs. Holt shooed the young girl away. "Come back later to clean up, Helen," she ordered.

As soon as the girl was gone, Mrs. Holt shook her finger at me. "Now let me tell you something. I ain't interested in seein' none of you Thatchers ever again, and that goes double for Addis. Now your ma's got her precious son back, she can keep him."

Mrs. Holt turned away so abruptly, her skirts caught on the edge of a chair. She quickly smoothed them down, but not before I'd seen her old, grubby slippers and dirty, ripped stockings. I laughed out loud. Mrs. Holt may have looked fancier on the outside, but she was as filthy as the rest of us underneath.

Luckily when I got back to our wagon, Addis was still asleep. Good, I could put off telling him for a while and in the meantime, I'd take a nap myself. After keeping watch all night, I was really tired.

I must have drifted right off. I remembered standing under a sparkly waterfall, letting its fresh clean spray splash through my fingers and fill my open mouth. Then I was aware of footsteps running, voices yelling, laughter. From a far distance, I heard the words that must have started me dreaming of water in the first place.

"Water! They've found water ahead!"

I lay in my tent without moving. I didn't want to open my eyes for fear I'd find out it was just a dream after all. Someone fired a rifle nearby. Others picked up the signal and all over camp I heard gunshots. Now I knew I was really awake.

I kicked off my quilt and scrambled out of the tent. The camp had gone wild. Men were dancing crazy jigs. Children pummeled and chased each other. Women cried in each other's arms. Caught up in the excitement, the dogs barked and ran in frantic circles. It was hard to believe, but it was true. A creek of fresh water had been found up ahead. We were saved. We could move out and leave Lost Hollow forever.

Everyone wanted to be on their way, and it was bedlam. The livestock were so scattered, rounding them up took hours. Pa hurried to finish repairs on our wagon. People were dumping as much cargo as they could to lighten their loads.

We all worked with renewed energy. I even heard old Mr. Walter saw away on his fiddle. I was in charge of the cooking utensils. After I'd scrubbed and dried them, I carried them into the wagon for packing. Ma had already told Addis the good news. As soon as he saw me, he tried to sit up, his bandaged head giving him a lopsided look.

"Didn't you tell Sophie I wanted to see her?"

In my excitement about leaving, I'd forgotten all about Sophie Holt. "Oh, I did, Addis, but . . . but she wouldn't come. She said to say good-bye."

Addis blinked. "Good-bye?"

I wanted to tell Addis he was better off without her, that she'd taken up with some awful man as soon as Addis was out of sight. Most of all, I wanted to tell him she was frumpy and old and dyed her hair, for pity's sake. Instead I just shrugged my shoulders. "I'm sorry, Addis, but she sounded like she meant it."

Addis slumped back on his pillow, his face screwed up in a funny way and I suddenly realized he was trying not to cry. I quickly turned my back and started packing. Addis had seemed so grown up lately, it was hard to remember he was only sixteen.

I had avoided Yvette all day. Now we had to take down the tents together. We didn't talk, but our silence was awkward, instead of comfortable the way it used to be. I was glad when Mary Herren came running over and interrupted us. Her face was pink with pleasure.

"Oh, Ella Jane, ain't it wonderful how they found water? Bethie seems better, too, thanks to your mother, and now that we're on our way, I know everything will be fine, just like you said. That handsome David Pugh was the one who found water up ahead. He was jest ridin' along not really payin' much mind to anything when somethin' green in the cut of the mountain caught his eye. He rode over, an' sure enough, there was a creek that couldn't be seen from the valley floor. He came ridin' back here with the news as fast as he could."

I stared at Mary in astonishment. The creek was in a cut in the mountain that couldn't be seen from the valley floor? That was just where Yvette had said it would be.

"The creek is north, then northwest of here, past a ridge of volcanic mountains?" I asked Mary, already knowing the answer.

"That's right. Did somebody tell you?"

"Yes, somebody did." I spoke to Mary, but looked at Yvette. She was smiling as if she were pleased with herself, and I couldn't blame her.

Yvette had even drawn a map describing the exact location of the creek. I owed her an apology. Yvette had been trying to help us. She was leading Pa right to water. All my suspicions were silly nonsense. Well, everything would be different now we were leaving this miserable place. Yvette and I could be friends again. I smiled at her.

"I'm sorry I've been so out of sorts lately, Yvette. I guess I haven't been very pleasant to anyone, especially you."

Yvette nodded as if in agreement. "We should make peace. We've seen much suffering, and there is no telling what hardships lie ahead."

I wished Yvette hadn't said that. Our bad times were all behind us. They just had to be.

CHAPTER TWENTY-THREE

NOT ONE PERSON LOOKED BACK WITH regret as our wagons pulled out of Lost Hollow. It was about three in the afternoon, and the wind was as gusty as ever. Ashes from our dead campfires blew into little whirlwinds. Trash we'd left behind was caught up in the rolling tumbleweed. Piles of cargo lay everywhere, boxes, clocks, chairs, tables, crates, trunks. The teams were so weak, anything that could ease the load was left behind.

A row of magpies perched on the makeshift privies, as if waiting for us to be gone so they could start their feast. Turkey buzzards had already begun to pick through the remains of the campground. I even saw the tan flash of a coyote moving in to scavenge, its tail low and its nose close to the ground. Well, they were welcome to all of it and good riddance.

Mr. Meek was our pilot again. There was still some grumbling about him, but now we were all on the move again, most everyone seemed willing to forgive him. As for me, I cared never to lay eyes on the man again. In my mind, Stephen Meek and Lost Hollow were one and the same, and I shuddered at the thought of either.

It was a good twenty-five miles to the creek ahead. Though Ma packed bags of sand around Addis' head to cushion the bumping, we still had to travel slowly. Ma sat in the wagon with Addis, while Yvette and I rode Major and Campbell. Pa drove the teams as usual.

We headed due north, then northwest, passing the rimrock mountains and volcanic ridges that Yvette had described. I pointed them out to her with a grin. She nodded and reined Major over so that we were riding side by side. We walked our horses in a companionable silence the rest of the afternoon, just like we used to. Dusk fell quickly. The stars came out, and then, near midnight, the moon rose, turning the gray desert into silvery shadows. We were traveling so slowly, we had dropped behind the main caravan, though for once it didn't bother me. There were other stragglers, and the wagons ahead had lit sagebrush fires as beacons to guide our way.

It was after two in the morning when we finally reached the creek. Smelling the water before they saw it, our teams practically charged the last one hundred yards. As soon as Pa unhitched them, they plunged into the water up to their necks. We all howled with laughter at the sight.

The second day's travel took us northwest. As the morning passed, the road became rockier and steeper. At every bump, our springless wagon bounced, forcing us to travel slower and slower to spare Addis. By noontime, we were a couple of miles behind the others. A scout from the main caravan reported back to us that the wagons were nooning up ahead by a creek. Pa wanted to keep going, but Addis was complaining of such a headache, Ma insisted we stop.

"If we go west a-ways, we will find water," Yvette called out to Pa. "It is only a short cutoff."

Oh, no, not another cutoff. "Let's camp here, Pa," I urged.

"Why should we settle for a dry camp when there's water nearby?" Pa argued. "Yvette's been right about where to find water so far."

I couldn't quarrel with that. Still, we'd had enough trouble with cutoffs to last forever. "Dry camp isn't so bad, Pa. We got plenty of water in the keg from last night."

Pa wouldn't hear of it. Nothing would do but we follow Yvette's directions and travel due west a fifth of a mile or so. Once we were camped, I felt better. Fresh water did sound good. Keg water was always warm and tasted faintly of the vinegar that had once been stored in it. And I had never been so dirty. I smelled from riding Campbell all morning, and my hair was caked with dust. I knew Addis would be pleased with fresh water, too. He'd done nothing but fret since we left Lost Hollow. Though he claimed his head hurt, I figured what Mrs. Holt had done hurt him even more.

"You and Yvette fetch the water while I start the campfire, Ella Jane," Pa ordered.

We each took a blue water bucket and started off for the creek. It was a beautiful day and blissfully peaceful after the hullabaloo of Lost Hollow. We had the whole world to ourselves. It felt like fall now. The sky was clear and bright, without the awful heat of the past few weeks. Overhead an eagle glided silently, his head and tail dazzling white as his shadow moved over the rocks. In every direction, the stark rimrock mountains etched black silhouettes against the blue sky.

We had walked a fair distance from the wagon when Yvette pointed down a steep ridge. A narrow creek ran through a ravine two hundred feet or so below us. I looked down at the rocky incline and hesitated. My leg was certainly better, but I wasn't sure it was up to that kind of effort.

"Let me carry your bucket," Yvette offered.

"I'll come only if you promise to kill the rattlesnakes," I said, only half-joking as I handed Yvette my bucket. This country looked like it would be crawling with snakes.

"There are no rattle-snakes here," Yvette reassured me.

I started my slow way down behind Yvette. She fairly ran, leaping from rock to rock as nimble as a mountain goat. Stones, loosened by our descent, tumbled down the incline, bouncing higher and higher until they splashed in the creek at the bottom.

Then we were at the bottom, too. The creek was only a couple of feet wide and about six inches deep, but it bubbled and ran as clear as crystal. I bent down for a drink, wheezing and panting. The altitude must be very high in these mountains for me to be so winded. When I had caught my breath, I rinsed my hands and face, then took off my shoes and stockings and waded into the ice-cold water.

"We can bathe," Yvette suggested.

Cold or not, a bath sounded good. I unbuttoned my dress and took it off. I would love to throw the filthy rag away, but instead, I folded and laid it on the bank. Dressed only in my petticoat, I eased into the freezing water slowly. But the bottom of the creek was rocky and uncomfortable, and I was sitting on a sharp stone. I reached under me for it and threw it aside. It didn't help. The whole creek was filled with sharp rocks just like the first. I got up and cleared a space free of rocks where I could sit. Then I dug out the gravel under the rocks down to the sandy bottom.

Something glittery in the sand attracted my eye. It was a shiny pebble, bright as brass, about the size of my smallest fingernail. I picked it up and examined it. The rays of the sun winked off its wet surface. Maybe there were more of these pretty yellow stones. I cleared away more rocks and scooped up a handful of gravel and sand from the water. Sure enough, there were lots of these little yellow grains mixed in with the gravel and sand, though none as big as the first.

Yvette had been watching. Now she came over to join me. The thin scar over her eyes pulled together and her face looked serious. She kneeled down in the shallow water, dug into the bottom of the creek and came up with her cupped hands full of gravel and sand just like I had. Here and there sparkled shiny yellow grains. One pebble was bigger than the rest, about the size of mine. Yvette dried it off and studied it, turning it over and over. Now she looked more than serious. She looked solemn.

"What is it, Yvette?"

Yvette held up the pebble between her thumb and forefinger. "It is gold."

For a minute I didn't understand what she had said. I just stared at her. Gold?

It was as if I had asked the question aloud. "It is gold," Yvette repeated.

I looked down again at the pebble in my own hand. Then I closed my fist around it as if to keep it safe. I had never seen gold before, but somehow I knew Yvette was right. These pebbles were gold, and the creek bed was full of them.

CHAPTER TWENTY-FOUR

K AK-KAK-KAK!''
I jumped. The air was so still, the call of the eagle above us was
shrill as a scream. I watched him soar on the air currents as I tried
to take in what had happened. Gold. It was too amazing to be true.

Yvette smiled as if my happiness made her happy. I grinned
back at her. Gold would give us everything we ever wanted. Pa
could buy decent tools and livestock and more milk cows. We could
build a handsome frame home instead of just a log house, and we
could send money back to Lucy and Benton and Grandma Fleming.

"Quick, Yvette, fill your bucket. We can sort out the gold from
the gravel later," I ordered as I began to dump as much sand and

144

gravel into my bucket as I could. I laughed with pleasure. "You'll be rich, too."

Yvette shrugged her shoulders. "Gold means nothing to me. I care about it only for you."

I looked at her in surprise. Yvette didn't understand. "Everything's changed now," I tried to explain. "With all the emigrants settling in the Oregon country, you'll need regular money and gold to buy things. Shell money and simple trading won't do any more."

Yvette glanced at my half-filled bucket. She nodded thoughtfully. Then she bent over and slowly began to fill her own bucket. I could see the ridge of her backbone through her dress. She looked thin, as if she had lost weight. Still, instead of complaining, she had helped me with my leg, and healed Ma. She had done so much for us. Why, if it hadn't been for Yvette and her cutoff, we never would have found this gold. I reached over and threw my arms around her.

"Oh, Yvette, if you knew how silly I've been, imagining all sorts of terrible things about you. Forgive me."

Yvette didn't resist my hug, but she didn't return it either. She stayed perfectly still, the way Sparky used to before she was tame. After a minute, I felt foolish and dropped my arms. Only then, when Yvette turned to face me, did I see the tears in her dark eyes. I was surprised. I had never known Yvette to cry before. Then her mouth curved up in a smile, and she tossed her thick braid over her shoulder.

"The gold will change everything, Ella Jane," she said.

"Oh, Yvette, it will change everything. Maybe now Addis will even forget that awful Mrs. Holt." I stopped as I realized it was the first time Yvette had ever called me Ella Jane. In fact, I didn't remember her ever calling any of us Thatchers by name. That was strange, considering she'd once said names were important to a Chinook. Well, what did it matter?

I filled my bucket first, and started up the rocky incline. Climbing up was a lot harder than getting down. I had to hold onto my skirts and carry the bucket as well. And the bucket was heavy, very heavy. I had to stop and catch my breath. I set my bucket on a rock, then sat down beside it. I held my face up to the sun for warmth. I was cold from being in the freezing creek water so long. I watched Yvette start up behind me. I waved, and though I knew she saw me, she didn't wave back.

"We must keep going. Your mother will be concerned," she said when she reached me. She put her bucket down by mine.

"Ma won't care when she sees what we found. Here, sit with me a spell while I rest."

Yvette shook her head so hard, her braid swung back and forth. "Non, we have to go on." She sounded angry.

"There's no hurry." My leg hurt, and I wanted to warm myself a little longer in the sun. Besides, it didn't make any difference. When Pa saw our gold, we wouldn't be moving on anyway.

Yvette tugged at my sleeve. "Come, we must go."

We wouldn't be moving on anyway. Of course we wouldn't. Pa would want to dig for as much gold as he could, and Pa was never any good at keeping secrets. He was bound to brag about the gold to his friends, and those friends would tell more friends. In no time at all, the whole caravan would hear about the gold. Everyone would want to stop and get their fair share. Why, we might be delayed here for days digging for gold. I looked down at the narrow little creek. It certainly wasn't big enough to provide water for our two hundred wagons and all the livestock. We couldn't afford to lay over now anyway, not when everyone's food supplies were so low.

"I don't know, Yvette. Maybe showing Pa this gold isn't such a good idea after all," I said.

Yvette frowned. "We have to. It's important."

A gust of wind blew through the ravine, picking up my skirts and bouncing a ball of tumbleweed past us. It was a chilling wind. We were high in these mountains. Even Pa said the first snows weren't far off. If we stopped now, we might be trapped by a snow-storm and never get out. That decided me. I stood up.

"I've made up my mind. The gold's not as important as our getting to The Dalles as fast as we can. I don't think we should say a word to Pa about it."

Yvette was almost trembling. "We have to tell your father."

"I thought you cared nothing for the gold at all."

"I don't. It is for you, and you must have it." Blue veins stood out on Yvette's hands where she clenched them into fists.

"If it's for me, then it shouldn't matter to you what I do with it." I reached down for my bucket and got a good grip on the handle. With one big swing, I tossed everything out of the bucket. The effort threw me off balance and I almost fell. I righted myself just in time to see the sand and gravel and gold scatter down the mountainside.

"Come on, Yvette, throw your gold away, too."

"Non." Yvette's eyes blazed almost ebony black, and I realized she was determined to take the gold back to our wagon. Well, if she wasn't going to get rid of it, I would. But Yvette must have guessed what I was thinking. She grabbed for her bucket just as I did. My hand closed over the handle first. I yanked her bucket off the ground and heaved it down the rocky incline. With a cry of protest, Yvette lunged to stop me, but her feet shot out from under her and she fell. Even as Yvette tumbled and slid, I saw her blue bucket shatter on the rocks below. Then Yvette was rolling over and over, faster and faster. In a quick motion, she reached up and grabbed the low-hanging branch of a stunted cedar tree. It stopped her fall with a jerk.

She lay still a moment. Then, as I scrambled down the incline toward her, she looked up. Her face was scratched and scraped raw on one cheek. I didn't notice that as much as her terrible expression of rage. A string of curses couldn't have said more. Yvette was furious at me beyond words. She didn't want me to help her. She didn't want me near her. I stopped short, ten feet or so above her.

147

"Are you all right, Yvette?"

"You have ruined it for me. Now the wagons will move on." Yvette's voice crackled with anger.

What an astounding thing to say. Yvette must have wanted our wagons to stop here. "I don't understand, Yvette. If we stop to dig for gold, we could be trapped by the snows. You want that?"

"Yes."

Though her answer was only a whisper, I was as stunned as if she had screamed it. That was the reason Yvette had been so anxious to show the gold to Pa. She wanted us to go crazy over the gold so we'd delay here . . . run out of supplies and water . . . get caught in the snows. Why, she must have known this gold was here and deliberately led us to it.

"Yvette, I can't believe you'd try to harm us when we took you in like family."

Yvette stared up at me from where she lay on the ground. One of the scratches on her face was bleeding, but she didn't move. Neither did I, as I waited for her explanation. It was as if our eyes were held together by an invisible cord. I wasn't aware of anything but the chill wind and the distant shadow of the eagle still sailing overhead.

"At first I had no regrets." Yvette's voice was low. "It was easy to turn your father against you, and your mother against your brother. Then time passed. You were fair to me, and trusted me. Still . . . I had to stop your wagons. I had to."

So Yvette had planned for Ma and me to come on Addis and Mrs. Holt, just like Addis thought. She'd set me up in that lie to Pa, too. And I remembered it was Yvette who had first compared Lucy to Mrs. Chambers and got Ma all upset. Yvette was the hex on this cutoff, not the Malheur River. My eyes spilled over with sudden tears, and I impatiently brushed them away.

"You must hate us."

Yvette was probably laughing at my tears right now. But she

148

wasn't laughing. She looked close to tears herself. "Hate has nothing to do with it. I didn't want to hurt you."

"Then why did you?" I shouted. "Sparky, you took my Sparky, didn't you? And Ma's Liberty Chest and Pa's rifle. Why? Why?"

Yvette was still looking right into my eyes. "To capture another's prized belonging is to gain that person's power. I had to have that power over you, but I failed."

I knew I should hate Yvette for what she'd done, but I couldn't. My anger was suddenly gone. Even thinking about Sparky only made me sad. "Tell me why you did it, Yvette," I said. "I have to know."

Yvette half-closed her heavy lids and broke the eye connection between us. "It is over. I must go."

She got slowly to her feet, and brushed off her raw and bleeding hands. Now she wouldn't look at me at all. Instead, she turned and started back down the mountain toward the creek. She moved quickly. Her slender feet leapt from stone to stone, her heels never touching the ground. I had seen her run that graceful way so often, I could hardly bear to watch her.

She had reached the bottom. She waded across the creek and started up the other side of the ravine. I wondered if the two Chinooks were waiting for her there. If they were, I didn't want to see them. I turned away and started up my side of the ravine, back toward our wagon.

If only Yvette had told me why she'd betrayed us, but she hadn't. I'd have to figure it out myself. But not now. I couldn't even think straight now. Later . . . I'd put my mind to it later.

CHAPTER TWENTY-FIVE

ALL I TOLD MA AND PA WAS THAT Yvette didn't want to go to the mission school, so she'd run off with two Chinooks who had been following us. That was true enough. Ma, especially, was upset, but there wasn't anything she could do about it. Yvette was gone, and we had to move on to keep up with the other wagons.

For the next few days, I did all my chores and helped with Addis, but I was as numb as a sleepwalker. I couldn't get Yvette out of my mind. Remembering her tears when I had hugged her, and how she had called me "Ella Jane," I knew in my heart she wasn't wicked. That she had tried to destroy our whole caravan just didn't make sense.

A couple of days after Yvette had left, I decided to go visit Mary Herren for something to do. I was walking from our wagon to hers when I heard a great honking and gabbling. I looked up. A flock of huge geese was flying overhead in a wavering V, their voices like a freedom call from the skies. As I stopped to watch the endless southward flight of them, I noticed they were descending. Maybe they were coming down to feed.

POOWW!

I heard a gunshot. Then another. A bird dipped, tried to fly on, then plunged to the ground. More shots rang out. I should have been pleased. Geese were good eating, but these birds were somehow too wild and free to be killed.

I covered my ears against the sound of the shooting, and looked away from the birds. My eyes fell on the rimrock mountain to the right of the path. Why, there was someone up there on the ledge. I shaded my eyes against the glare of the sun. The figure was half-hidden by a cedar tree, but it appeared to be a woman, an Indian woman. She faced north, looking down at our wagons circling for noon camp. Though her back was to me, I realized she was too small for a woman. It was a girl. Then she took a few steps forward, and as soon as I saw the graceful way she moved, I knew it was Yvette.

She must have been following us. Maybe she wanted to see me. I certainly wanted to see her. For my peace of mind, she just had to answer the questions that had been bothering me. I'd climb up on that ledge right now and settle everything once and for all. Ma thought I was on my way to the Herrens' wagon, and the Herrens didn't know I was coming. No one would miss me.

Scrubby sage and cedars grew in the shaly rock at the base of the mountain. I darted behind a clump of sagebrush and started up. The mountain wasn't steep and I carried a walking stick that helped. Still, I was winded by the time I reached the ledge, and I knew that was from more than just the climb. I was suddenly shy about meeting Yvette face to face.

She was still looking north toward our camp. She didn't see me. Good. That gave me a chance to catch my breath, and get used to her strange clothing. She wore a cape of rabbit skins and a beautiful fringed skirt of some kind of silky fiber that reached to her knees. Though her feet were bare, tight cords were tied around both ankles. Her hair was cut short, to ear lobe level, and it blew loose in the unexpectedly fierce wind that swept across the ledge.

"Yvette." It was hard for me to get the word out.

She spun around. I don't know who was more startled, Yvette or me. Her face was powdered chalk white. Red ochre, bright as blood, covered the part in her hair and decorated her eyebrows. I remembered when Mrs. Chambers had died, Yvette had told me how the Chinooks painted their faces white when there was a death. Yvette was in mourning. But who had died?

Yvette recovered first. She shook her head so hard her hair blew across her face. "I am no longer Yvette. I am Masasa, daughter of Coyote, the swift runner."

Masasa. I'd never forget that name or the night she took it. Still, I couldn't bring myself to call her that. It was hard enough to look at her painted face.

"Tell me . . . I . . . I have to know . . . why you wanted to destroy us and the other wagons . . ." I was almost stuttering. Yvette's eyes were shiny black pebbles in her ghostly face as she scowled at me.

I could never tell what Yvette was thinking. Maybe she was considering my question, or maybe she was deciding whether to answer at all. The wind was blowing so hard, I had to lean on my walking stick for support. Yvette's hair fanned straight out, but she stood sturdy as a tree. She finally raised her hands palms up and I knew she was going to speak.

"My grandfather Dusdaq cast out my mother from the tribe. My mother doesn't care, but I am a Chinook, and I care. To return to the tribe as a member I had to prove myself worthy."

152

I waited. I knew Yvette well enough not to hurry her. I even tried to smile encouragement, but it came out more of a grimace.

"My grandfather sent Tskiluks and Qatqos to test me," she went on. "If there was difficulty, they were prepared to help." Again she stopped, this time as if she were finished.

Those must be the two Chinooks who had followed us. But Yvette still hadn't answered my question. "We never hurt you. Why should hurting us get you back in the tribe?"

"Do you recall the tale of the Raven?"

I nodded. "He was greedy," I answered in my stupid little-girl voice.

"My people want only what is theirs. Your people, like Raven, are not satisfied with what they have been given. They want more than their share. See how they shoot our birds."

"We need the geese for food. You know our supplies are low," I argued. "Besides, your father isn't Chinook. Why should you turn against your father's people?"

"You do not understand. The white race has so vast a number, they have no need of me. The Chinooks are few, and every person is of great value."

"But we've tried to help you in every way we could. We've opened schools and doctored your sick, and sent missionaries to Christianize you . . ."

"No more!" Yvette cried out. "You still do not understand. It is the halo wind for my people. See." She swept her arm out over the valley below us.

For the first time, I took my eyes off Yvette and stepped past her, closer to the edge. The wind was so strong, I had to brace myself against the rock face of the cliff as I looked down.

Our caravan sprawled as far as the eye could see. At least a hundred wagons had coiled into separate circles for the nooning camp with horses hobbled inside the circles. Outriders were driving the livestock to water in a billowing cloud of dust. A single line of wagons straggled into the main camp. There was our wagon. Ma, carrying her faded black umbrella against the sun, rode Campbell, while Pa walked behind Jackson and Ben. Another group of wagons, maybe fifteen or twenty, had already started on their afternoon trek.

The wagon covers blossomed across the valley like a huge field of white poppies. The north wind carried the smell of dust and campfires and burning sagebrush and cooking food up to us. The wind carried the noise as well, the bawling of cattle, hammering and sawing as men made repairs, gunshots, and the clatter of iron-tired wagon wheels over the rocky terrain.

I was amazed. I had never seen our wagons from high up like this, an eagle view of it all. Our caravan with its dust and noise and smells had swallowed up the whole countryside. It was like an invasion. We were a huge, moving, unstoppable force spreading out over the land. Yvette had realized from the beginning that our coming meant the end for her people, and she had done her best to stop us.

I could never accept how she had tried to destroy our wagons, but at least I understood now why she had done it. And why she was in mourning. I turned to tell her, but she was gone. All that was left was the wind whistling through the branches of the cedar tree. It was almost as if she had never been.

ALTHOUGH ELLA JANE THATCHER, her family and Yvette Dumelle are fictional characters, the incident of the Meek cutoff really took place. In 1845, Stephen Meek led approximately one thousand emigrants onto a short cut from the regular Oregon road. They were soon lost in the high desert country of central Oregon. Seven weeks later the exhausted survivors staggered into The Dalles mission. At least twenty-four people died as a result of their ordeal, possibly as many as fifty. Despite the number of dead, only one tombstone marks the Meek cutoff, young Sarah Chambers' grave near Castle Rock (mistakenly called Fremont's Peak by the emigrants).

Gold was supposedly found in a creek bed during the lost caravan's wanderings, some three years before gold was discovered in California. Expeditions later went out to find the gold but none were successful. Unfortunately, the lost emigrants were never able to retrace their exact route, so that the legend of Blue Bucket gold has persisted in Oregon lore to this day.

What about the Indians? Although the Oregon country did not become a United States territory until 1848, American settlers, streaming in from the east, coveted the rich Willamette Valley south of the Columbia River. By 1845, the year the white population of the Oregon country doubled from three thousand to six thousand, the Chinook population had already dropped significantly. The broken treaties, Indian wars and massacres that followed the settling of the west are well known. The push to expand westward and control the whole continent, our Manifest Destiny as it was called in the nineteenth century, sounded the death knell to the self-determination and independence of the American Indian.